**monsoon**books

S0-BLA-174

# LOCKED OUT

Alison Jean Lester was born and educated in the United States, and has lived in the UK, Italy, China, Taiwan, Japan and now Singapore. In spite of her Master's degree in Chinese studies and economics, Lester works as a communication coach, writer and improvisational comedian. She has two extremely amusing children and is herself the great great great-granddaughter of Phiz (Hablot Knight Browne, Charles Dickens's illustrator) and the daughter of author Valerie Lester and author and jazz musician James Lester.

She has written for *The Los Angeles Times*, *Asian Business*, *Canadian*, *Modern Maturity*, *The Japan Times Weekly*, *Tokyo Journal*, *Today's Parents*, *The Straits Times*, *Elvis Monthly*, *Wingspan* and other publications. This is her first book.

# Locked Out

## STORIES FAR FROM HOME

ALISON JEAN LESTER

monsoon

**monsoon**books

Published in 2006
by Monsoon Books Pte Ltd
106 Jalan Hang Jebat #02–14, Singapore 139527
www.monsoonbooks.com.sg


ISBN-13: 978-981-05-5300-5
ISBN-10: 981-05-5300-5

Frontcover photograph©James Lester, 2006




Printed in Singapore

10 09 08 07 06          1 2 3 4 5 6 7 8 9

In memory of Midori Yoshida

# Contents

Locked Out — 11

Bill's Bones — 35

My Thing — 73

Needing Ice — 81

Being Japanese — 97

Tiptoe — 107

Strays — 139

Singapore Sting — 161

The War Of The Worlds — 173

Really Trying To Get Somewhere — 179

# Locked Out

It was by far the hottest summer in the three years we'd been in Tokyo. I couldn't go out without feeling unequal to the challenge of getting back home. Even when I put the air conditioning on in the apartment, I could still hear the relentless mating calls of the cicadas outside—like chainsaws in a rain forest—reminding me of the intensity beyond the windows. Children went by in the mornings, dragging their feet and perspiring. I couldn't wait to see them skip and scuffle again in the fall. And what must it have been like for really old people? Every morning, all spring, there had been a woman across the road who pulled the few dozen hairs she had left into a tiny bun at the back of her head, opened her sliding door, put down a mat, and knelt to weed with chopsticks in her tiny garden of potted flowers. I hadn't seen her in weeks.

There were Sundays when it was almost too hot for our favorite weekend treat of crêpes in the Omotesando area of Tokyo. Some Japanese like to say that Omotesando is like the Champs Elysées in Paris. I don't know what they're talking about. Omotesando is shorter and narrower, and most of its charm is hidden in its side streets.

This was one of those hot Sundays. We had settled ourselves at Le Bretagne, and had been served our usual order of galettes and cider, when Hank said, "The people in the office think I'm sleeping with Ikeda-san." He related this as if it was supposed to be funny, but it was amazing how simultaneously my face felt hot and my heart felt cold. Maybe it wouldn't have been so bad if Natalie, who worked at Louis Vuitton, hadn't told me just the day before that her company's French president had given his rather severe wife the heave-ho in favor of a sparkling Japanese sales manager.

"Oh?" I said, forking some warm cheese and ham into our three-year-old son, Miller.

"Can you believe that?"

"Maybe," I said.

"She's a bit of a flirt, you know."

I looked at him. "I didn't know." Miller was losing interest in his food, so I let him shake some salt on it.

"Yeah," Hank continued, sitting back with a fresh cup of cider, easing into his story. His big, boyish face looked silly atop his broad chest and thick arms. "When she started she was making one of the other guys really uncomfortable by bringing him tea every morning and standing on tiptoe to adjust his tie and stuff."

"I thought that was their job."

"Not in foreign companies it isn't."

"That's good to hear."

Hank didn't seem to register the chill in my tone—he's used to me being a little sarcastic—and continued his story.

"Yeah. So when she came over to me, I told her she was being unprofessional."

"Can I play with the shoes, Mommy?" Miller asked.

"Sure, sweets," I said, wiping his face. He slid off his chair and headed for the wooden clogs artfully arranged in the corner of the room. "How'd she take it?" I asked Hank. I wasn't sure I was enjoying the conversation, but I was always quite fascinated by the ways Japanese women worked things out for themselves.

"She definitely looked shocked," he said. "And a little huffy. I guess I caused her to lose face."

He dug back into his food with enthusiasm, but I wasn't ready to do the same. "So why the rumor?"

"What?"

"Why do people think you're sleeping with her?"

"It gives them something to do?" he suggested.

I looked at him skeptically over the rim of my cup. "She's not even that pretty."

"No?" Hank looked very surprised to hear this, but then seemed to correct himself. "Look," he said, "she's only twenty-two. Her father probably never talks to her,

her mother's probably a grin-and-bear-it housewife. She's had no one to teach her how to behave in an office."

"Until now," I said, and we both looked out the window rather than at each other. On the sidewalk, a pair of well-dressed Japanese women with little designer handbags over their forearms wondered whether or not to brave this foreign restaurant. They caught sight of us staring at them and skittered away.

Hank shook his head. "It's just getting a little weird again. I think I'll try to find her a mentor."

We heard Miller shouting "I don't *like* you!" to someone in the corner, and Hank got up, leaving me alone with the dregs of my cider and a heart he had set spinning like a penny.

There was too much come and go for me in Tokyo. It took the first nine months to find Melitta, a German woman Miller and I met in a nearby playground. She and I used to have tea together a few times a week and share Japan survival tactics. When she had trouble during her second pregnancy, I looked after her little boy for a few days. It began to feel like I was living in a neighborhood rather than just on a street. Her husband's job suddenly took them to Paris, though. We wrote for a while, then she had a third child.

I liked Natalie, but she worked all the time. The women at the American Club—a sprawling complex cheek by jowl with the Russian Embassy, where we could laugh with our mouths wide open, order club sandwiches, put up signs when we wanted to sell our king-size comforters or exercise bicycles—were friendly and energetic, but since they always seemed to be striving so hard for their grim smiles, I didn't want to rain on their parades. There was a beautiful young Japanese woman living upstairs from us with her husband and two little boys, and sometimes I thought we could be friends. We were always meeting in the echoing marble entrance and calling to each other that we should get together soon (her English was letter perfect), though we hardly ever did. The one time she did manage to come by, I sat and envied her hair, her clothes, and her face, while she told me about the PhD she was hoping to do someday on the Japanese attitude toward the Jews. I don't remember what brought it on. She just seemed to be bursting with it, as if it were some sort of confession. I wasn't sure I could do that again.

A Korean family moved in next door sometime that spring. The wife's name was Sook Young. I only remembered because I made her write it down for me and had stuck it up on the kitchen wall. When I first saw her, with her heavy long hair pulled up and her mules and trendy dress, I immediately thought *bimbo*. She was unusually leggy, unusually voluptuous, and her fingers were long and strong. Soon afterward I heard the most beautiful music coming through her front door. It turned out that she was

15

singing it. *And* playing the piano.

Our kitchens were right next to each other, and every evening I heard her chopping away like crazy. Once I went over to see if she could spare an egg. She came to the door in an apron, with a shiny, sweating face and strands of hair like careless strokes of calligraphy on her cheeks and forehead. Her smile was so sweet, it was like one of those Japanese cartoons.

"Wow!" I said when Miller and I followed her into the kitchen. I was making a quiche, which I thought was pretty fancy until I saw what Sook Young was preparing. She'd just fried some chicken and placed it on a glass plate lined with lettuce. I could smell rice cooking. There was a salad and something dark green and fermented-looking already on the dining table.

"What are you making?" she asked me.

"Quiche," I answered.

"What is quiche?"

"Oh, it's kind of a cheesy pie. Eggs, milk, cheese, vegetables, maybe a little bacon or salmon. In a pie crust."

"And?"

"And?"

"Just quiche?"

"Yeah, just quiche."

She sighed. "You are so lucky."

"I am?"

"If I no put many dishes, my husband very unhappy. Is. Is very unhappy."

I studied her flushed face. "Every day?"

She nodded, sliding hairs away with the back of her hand.

"Yikes," I said.

She laughed and rubbed Miller on the head. She opened the fridge, releasing an aromatic cloud smelling of cold garlic, dried chili, and something between ginger and dirt. She found me an egg and slipped a chocolate into Miller's hand.

Back in our apartment, I tried to doll up my quiche with a ring of cucumber slices around the edge of the plate. I did feel lucky not to have to sweat it out in the kitchen for so long every night. But also a tad boring. I thought of all the places in the world where people paid so much more attention to detail than I did—the ash around the eyes, the bamboo stake through the lip, the beads and shells, the lingerie, the deliberate contrasts. You would never see a matched set of porcelain at a Japanese meal. Each plate or bowl was chosen for the way it suited the dish or tidbit being served. I could hardly look at my wedding china anymore, it was so monotonous. And when a woman put on a kimono, the obi she tied it with had to be made not only in a contrasting design but also of a contrasting fabric. Meanwhile I went around in navy slacks and a white shirt, and sometimes I remembered to change my earrings.

I saw Sook Young again on the following Saturday morning. I'd taken Miller out for a spin around our block of tightly packed apartment buildings on his tricycle. People rose late on the weekends, so there were few cars about. Sook Young was coming in from grocery shopping. I'd seen her husband driving off in a champagne-colored Jaguar earlier.

"Was that your car?" I asked her after I mentioned seeing him.

She shook her head. "Company car. My husband is playing golf with his boss."

"I see," I said. "That explains the amazing green shirt. Does he play a lot of golf?"

She thought for a moment. "Golf," she said. "Golf is . . . Golf is the other woman."

She smiled, so I laughed. "I guess having the Jaguar to drive on the weekends is no compensation."

It took her a little while to understand this, but then she nodded repeatedly. "No compensation," she said, enjoying the word. She said it again. "No compensation."

It was so easy to tell Hank I loved him. "Love you," we always said at the end of a call if I phoned him at the office. Another woman might have told her husband in the middle of sex, to increase the tenderness of the event, but I knew Hank didn't like to be interrupted. He was very hearty about his lovemaking, in a charming, prehistoric way. That night, though, he started to talk.

"You know what I like, Cath?" he asked between deep breaths, snatching me back to the present from a reverie about a high school biology teacher.

"Tell me," I replied warmly, astounded and aroused by this new intimacy.

"Slippers," he exhaled back.

"What?"

"Slippers," he said again. The word had apparently flipped his switch, and he was thrusting.

Before we fell asleep I turned to him. "Slippers, Hank?"

"Never mind," he said.

"What kind of slippers?"

"Forget it, okay?"

Hank's attention was in short supply in Tokyo, since he was so motivated about his work. We'd sit down to dinner and I'd see him shake his head a little as he lifted his fork. Sometimes his lips even moved.

"Who are you talking to?" I'd ask him, and he'd smile, but it wasn't enough to bring him all the way home.

So one morning, when it was clearly going to be unbelievably hot, I pulled out the shorts I'd been wearing when we met and put them on. I was already wearing my bathing suit, in anticipation of doing some laps at the American Club, but I had yet to throw on a top. I went out to the kitchen where Hank was making his morning coffee.

"Hey," I said.

"Hey," he said back, then did a double-take.

"Aren't those—?" he asked.

"Yeah," I said, smiling and doing a turn for him.

He poured his coffee, then looked at me again. "They're getting a little old, don't you think?"

"What do you mean?" I asked. I should have said yes. No, I should have said no and shut him up. Instead I had to ask him what he meant.

"Well, they just seem to have lost their shape a bit, that's all," he said, sipping. "Why don't you go out and get yourself a new pair?"

Ha ha. He had no idea what it was like for an American woman of average size to shop in a city like Tokyo. I was a size 10 at home, a perfect M in my opinion, but in a country where clothes were made for laxative-popping secretaries (excuse me, *assistants*) like Ikeda-san, I was huge. I'd been an extra large for three years.

"Fly me home," I told him.

"What?"

"Japanese clothes don't fit me, Hank. Not to mention the fact that they're ugly."

"They're not all ugly," he said.

"No? Where've you been shopping?"

"Come on, Cathy, this is a huge city. There must be

something big enough for you in it."

"I have better things to do with my time."

"Fair enough," he said, setting his coffee mug in the sink. This was office speak—how he talked to his employees. In his mind, Hank had already hit the road.

He kissed me on the cheek when he left, but kissed Miller on his Rice Krispie-flecked lips. I tried not to let it bother me, but it did. Poor Miller found out just how much when he went and poured himself some more apple juice just for the fun of pouring, then refused to drink it, right before we needed to leave the apartment to get him to day care.

"Drink it," I said.

He didn't move a muscle.

"Drink it," I said again, enunciating with menace.

He was a statue, staring at the table. Very impressive.

I picked up the little green cup and held it in front of his mouth. I should have softened here, but felt myself make the choice to go on. "If you aren't going to drink it," I told him, "don't pour it!" I slammed the cup back down on the word *pour*. The apple juice jumped up out of the cup and splashed onto Miller's shorts. The ball I was trapped in started rolling faster down its hill. I pointed to the front door. "Go and get your shoes on," I ordered.

Miller looked down at his wet shorts.

"Go!" I shouted. "Hurry up!" I pulled him out of his chair and pushed him toward his shoes. When I got him there, he finally started wailing in disbelief. He had a point. I hardly ever shouted at him. But I was lost, and started shoving his shoes on his feet.

"But my shorts are all wet, Mommy!" he sobbed. "I'm all *wet*!"

"And whose fault is that?" I hissed back. When I looked at his face I could see that he had quite logically worked out that it was my fault, so I quickly pressed on. "Okay, okay," I said resentfully, dragging his shorts down and unbalancing him so that he had to put his hands on my shoulders. I should have hugged him then. Instead, I got up and left him standing alone by the door in his little Thomas the Tank Engine underpants, and went to get him some clean shorts.

When I returned his face was wet with tears, and snot was creeping toward his top lip. I pulled the clean shorts on over his shoes and grabbed a tissue from the bathroom.

"Blow," I commanded, holding the tissue over his nose. He wouldn't. His big brown eyes stared at me. Tears had pulled his long eyelashes into shiny stars. "Blow," I said. "NOW!" We glared at each other. Part of me wanted to whack him so hard. Another part knew I should cuddle him and bleat apologies. Yet another part had nothing but admiration for his defiance in the face of my uncontrollable rage. I was desperate for him to obey me, but then again I would have hated my little boy to be afraid of me. The hell with it, I thought, and stuck the tissue in my waistband.

I reached for his backpack, shoved my feet into flip-flops, and pushed him out the door.

When it clicked behind me, I realized I'd left my keys inside.

"Oh, no," I said.

Miller blinked. "What, Mommy?" He could tell I wasn't focused on him anymore, and looked hopeful.

"I left my keys inside."

"That's okay," he said.

"Sure. Except that I can't get back in, can I?"

"Oh," he said. "Oh, no."

I deserved to be locked out. "Silly Mommy," I said.

Miller knew this was his key to smile again. "Silly Mommy!"

"Silly Mommy getting so angry she can't remember her keys." I picked him up and put him on my right hip, with his backpack over my left shoulder. "I'm so sorry, Miller," I said with my nose right up against his cheek. "I got too angry."

"That's okay," he said. "*Now* I'll blow my nose."

People simply did not walk down the streets of Tokyo—even the back streets—in bathing suits and shapeless shorts. This wasn't a terribly serious problem for me, though, since everything foreigners did was considered relatively strange. You could see it in their faces as you passed. It was like they were thinking, "That's *weird*! Oh, wait, she's a foreigner. Figures." Every once in a while you'd see a flash of "I wish I could do that" in their eyes, usually if it was winter and you'd put on a nice warm hat. This was a country where, not so long ago, they walked around all year in sandals and two-toed socks. When it snowed, they put the sandals on stilts. Drier, but still cold. So walking back home from the day care center in a Speedo wasn't a problem for me. What *was* embarrassing was standing outside my building with no keys.

I pressed Sook Young's buzzer, desperately dragging the depths of my brain for the correct pronunciation of her name.

"Oh!" she exclaimed when she saw me on the video intercom.

"I'm locked out," I said. "Can you let me in?"

"Yes," she said, and the doors slid open.

"Wait!" I shouted into the speaker, worried that she thought this was all I needed. "Can I come to your apartment?"

I heard her laugh. "Of course."

When she opened the door she laughed again, gesturing for me to come inside. Sometimes her English deserted her completely.

"May I use your phone?" I asked.

She pointed, then sat down to watch me.

I called Hank. I told him what had happened and said, "You've got your keys, right? Can I come and get them?"

"Sure," he said. Then he added, "Wait, let me think. Would it be better for you if I put them in a cab and asked the driver to take them over?"

"Too risky," I said. There were almost no such risks in Japan, but I wanted to inject myself into his day and get a better look at Ikeda-san. I wasn't going to let the opportunity slip away. "I'll be there in about a half hour."

"You have money?" he asked.

"I'll get some." Sook Young was smiling in such a friendly way that I knew this was true.

"See you in a bit, then," he said, and we hung up.

Sook Young sat up straight, as if ready for whatever I was going to say next.

"Can I take a shower?" I asked her. I'd worked up quite a sweat.

"Of course," she said, getting up.

I stood as well. "Can I borrow some clothes?"

She smiled. "Yes."

"Can I have some money?"

She laughed outright. "Anything," she said.

While I was in the shower, hoping that the woodsy-smelling goo I was putting on my hair was shampoo, she pulled out some clothes for me. She may have been Asian, but she was my size.

"You need underwear?" she called through the door.

25

"Um, actually, yes. Do you mind?"

In answer, the door opened a little bit and her hand came in, depositing a couple of lacy white garments on the edge of the sink. It entered again with a towel, then withdrew, at which point I stepped out and dried myself. Wrapped in the towel, I picked up her hairbrush, which was full of her long, unbelievably strong black hairs. This made me think of Ikeda-san. Her hair must feel like this, I thought. If Hank was having an affair, I could imagine strands of it between his thumb and index finger. Not pale brown (or, let's face it, occasionally white) like mine, but black and heavy and musky and young. I clawed Sook Young's hairs out of the brush and dropped them in the little plastic trash can.

When my own hair was brushed, I unwrapped myself from the towel and pulled on the panties Sook Young had chosen for me. I put my arms through the bra straps and leaned over to drop my breasts into the cups. Standing up to do the hook, I had a shock. I was beautiful.

"Is it okay?" Sook Young asked from beyond the door, which was still a little ajar.

"I look fabulous!" I called back and opened the door to step out.

"We are the same size!" she exclaimed, handing me some shorts and a light blue knitted top. "Don't worry," she added. "The underwear is new."

"Do I look worried?" I said, pulling on the very cute

khaki shorts. "Where did you buy them?"

"Isetan," she said. "Very cheap."

I loved this. Most people in Japan didn't like to talk about how cheaply they bought stuff. In fact, according to Natalie, despite the still-struggling economy, Louis Vuitton had never done better.

I pulled on the top, and we both looked at me in the mirror of her vanity table.

"I feel like I'm in college again," I said.

She smiled and nodded at my reflection. "I'm never bored with you." She handed me a five-thousand-yen bill at the door. I couldn't bring myself to borrow shoes as well, so I put on my flip flops and went out into the heat.

In the back of the cool taxi I felt like a million bucks. In my mind I was full of youthful irresponsibility, and I was on my way to surprise my boyfriend. I planned how I'd step into Hank's office, turn my back on his busy colleagues and flash him a view of the lacy bra I was wearing.

When we arrived I got out of the taxi, laughed at the ugly clothes in the window of the designer boutique—Hanae Mori just wouldn't quit it with the bias cuts and the butterflies—and got in the elevator. The blood in my body felt like sap rising. I breezed past the uniformed receptionist, walked down the hall and turned the corner. Hank saw me through his window and nodded at me to come in. When I opened the door I saw that he was talking to Ikeda-san.

Even though she was reclining in her chair, her back was poker straight, pushing her little apple breasts up and slightly out of her fancy black tank top. Her hands gripped the arms of the chair, and her legs were crossed. The tension in the room made it hard to breathe. Hank looked like a coil of steel.

"Here's the other woman I sleep with," he said to Ikeda-san.

He thought he was joking, but I didn't laugh and Ikeda-san didn't move a muscle. She kept looking at him as if he were going to tell her what she should do. There was definitely some satisfaction in watching him struggle between wanting to guide Ikeda-san in the right direction and wondering what I was going to do as I towered over her. I considered breaking her arm, not because I thought she had seduced my husband—I wasn't sure about that— but because it would have been so easy to do. I feel the same way about Chihuahuas.

"Nice to see you again," I finally said, holding out a hand in a way that would force her to stand up to shake it. I could have bowed slightly, and she could have bowed back, but I thought she should get up.

She did. "Nice to see you again, too," she said, and we shook. Her hand was limp and cold and damp, and submitted to the force of mine as if it were holding its breath and praying for deliverance. How could this person have been attractive? Why was submission better than enthusiasm?

At this point I knew that, having performed our ritual, we were supposed to turn back to Hank, but I wasn't ready. "How are you?" I asked, looking her up and down. That was when I noticed her slippers, their little embossed bears staring me cheekily in the face. Where I came from, women wore sneakers for the commute and pumps for the office. In Tokyo they wore heels for the folks on the subway and slippers for the boss. No wonder the men went crazy. These women looked ready for bed at all hours.

"Fine, thank you," she answered, and tried once again to turn to Hank.

"Nice shoes," I said.

She giggled, a little confused, but clearly relieved that I was keeping things mundane.

"Do you have different styles, depending on your outfit, or maybe what mood you're in?"

"Cathy," Hank interrupted, "I think Ikeda-san has things to do."

"Oh, sure. You bet. Sorry. Don't let me keep you."

She left. Hank got up to close the door behind her.

"What the hell was that?" he demanded, turning on me like a bull.

"Is Ikeda-san's bra padded?"

"What?"

"It looks like it to me."

He threw up his arms. "How would I know?"

"Give me the keys, Hank."

"No. What's going on?"

I put out a hand.

He reached into his pocket, looking extremely confused.

"Thanks," I said when he'd laid the keys on my palm, warm from his heavy thigh. I turned and put a hand on the door.

"Wait," he said.

I stopped and looked back. His face reminded me of the way he'd behaved when we started dating, when he really wanted to kiss me.

"You look great," he said. "Where'd you get those clothes?"

"Sook Young," I responded flatly.

"They fit you really well."

"You're surprised?" I still had my hand on the door, but I turned my body a bit toward him.

"I thought you said Japanese clothes didn't fit you."

"Sook Young is Korean."

"Oh," Hank said, nodding. "Uh-huh."

He was looking at my breasts, staring at them like a thirteen-year-old. His mouth was actually hanging open. I watched a hard-on point to the space his keys had left, then begin to fill it. I had known in the taxi that I was going to turn him on. I had been on the war path, and I'd scalped the enemy. But now all I could think was, *Next time, remind me to marry a grown-up.*

"Think she'd let you have the shorts?" he said.

I looked down at Sook Young's clothes. My old red shorts reminded me of the volleyball I used to play, and outlet shopping in Maine. Although Sook Young's clothes flattered me, they carried her physical memories. "I don't want her shorts, Hank," I told him, and left.

Standing on the sidewalk just outside the door to Hank's building, I watched the people go by. It was late morning now, and well-turned-out ladies were climbing out of taxis and paying for exorbitantly priced cups of tea in preparation for visiting Prada, Moschino, Issey Miyake, Max Mara. There were young women on the street as well. Two had painted their faces white with black lines like cracks down their cheeks. One was dressed like a doll in a pinafore and knee socks. She had ribbons in her hair and carried a basket. After a few moments, along came a trio of girls in their early twenties who had clearly made their own clothes. The sun glinted off the shiny threads of the vibrant old kimonos they had cut up to fashion a pair of bell-bottomed pants, a dramatically long jacket, and a miniskirt with a bustle. Some of their hair blew around their necks, the rest was piled in stiff mounds and secured by traditional ornaments—spikes of metal topped with dangling butterflies and flowers in that characteristically Japanese combination of delicacy and danger.

Clearly there was a whole lot more room for imagination

in my wardrobe. I had options I'd never considered. But I found I didn't care. The adrenalin was draining out of my body, and the morning's excitement was becoming a colorful snapshot I'd paste in my memory album with the caption: *Not me at all.*

Suddenly I missed Miller, with an ache I knew I didn't have to question. I made my way across the wide sidewalk and hailed a cab, asking the driver to take me home. I only said home because I didn't know how to tell him in Japanese to take me to the day care center. I'd walk from the apartment. No, I'd run. I couldn't wait to see my little boy. He'd be happy to see me, too. When we walked back to the apartment I'd carry him for a little while, and he'd probably pull my hair and say, "Giddyup!" Giddyup I would. It wouldn't matter what I was wearing. Miller liked my simple outfits just fine.

# *Bill's Bones*

On June 6th, 1999, Judith Reynolds wrote to Club Med in Paris from her home north of Sydney. Somewhere in the desk was one of her husband's cigars. She hadn't been able to find it yet, but she could smell it. Her nostrils flared. She wrote:

*Dear Club Med,*

*I know that you must seldom, if ever, consider applications from middle-aged people, but please make me an exception.*

*I have been teaching primary three children for the last twelve years. My own children are now teenagers, and it is time they saw the back of me for a bit. More than that, I wish I had raised them differently. I wish our home had been more like Club Med.*

*So I am offering myself as an employee in your Petit Club Med. I enclose my resume. I have spent the last three weeks writing it. It is my first.*

*Perhaps, as you read it, you will find that my name rings a bell. Reynolds. It was my husband of twenty years, Bill Reynolds, who drowned in the surf at your resort at Ria Bintan, Indonesia, on Boxing Day last year. The search for his body was unsuccessful. Since then, I've been remembering how, several days before Christmas, one of our boys went body surfing and lost his goggles in a big wave. The water was so tumultuous and so full of sand that he quickly abandoned his search for them. The following day he entered the water and stepped right on them. I remember the look on his face as he retrieved them with his big toe and turned around to show me.*

*If Bill had surfaced, I know you would have contacted me, as we agreed. He might still do so. I'm not sure I can bear the thought of not being there when he does.*

*Not that I entirely regret his death. He gave me a bash on the face on Christmas night that I had to cover with sunglasses and a floppy hat on Boxing Day. That morning I felt him kiss the swollen eye before I heard him go out the door. Claudia, our youngest, on the balcony of the adjoining room, saw him go under and not come up.*

*Please give serious consideration to this letter. Please let me work at Bintan.*

*Yours very sincerely,*
*Judith Reynolds*

Paris passed the letter to Singapore operations. The Singapore office discussed the possibility of letting Mrs. Reynolds live free of charge at Club Med Ria Bintan for, say, a week a year. Marketing squelched the idea: not keeping her busy might lead to too much poolside or barside discussion of her husband's demise. Someone in finance quipped that giving her too sweet a deal might lead to a rash of women pushing their husbands into the monsoon-churned sea. The chief counsel kept saying that because it was well-posted that there was no lifeguard on the beach and that guests swam at their own risk, Club Med had no legal obligation to act.

But the Senior Vice President of Operations, Danesh Rupani, had sped to the resort at the news of the drowning. He remembered the woman, her sunglasses, her floppy hat, the two silent boys and the tall, bespectacled girl who had seen her father disappear. Correctly judging that Judith Reynolds would be offended by the rolling out of a red carpet, he pushed Paris for approval and dispatched his response on July 12th:

*Dear Mrs. Reynolds,*

*Thank you for your letter of application. I was pleased to hear from you, although distressed to be reminded of your family's tragedy.*

*Your concern that we tend to employ younger, single*

*people is well-placed. However, your resume is indeed impressive. You have clearly taken a good deal of initiative in your work. In addition, your familial obligations are clearly lessening, and your experience suits our needs.*

*We would be pleased to consider you for a position in our Petit Club, in charge of the four- to six-year olds.*

*Under normal circumstances, you would be directed to interview at our Australian office. If you can bear the expense, however, I would be delighted to interview you here at my office in Singapore.*

*My very best wishes as you decide what to do.*

*Sincerely,*
*Danesh Rupani*

Reading this letter, Judith nodded twice. Usually flustered in the face of such respectful kindness (her father had been as forceful as Bill, with a redder face), this time she thought to herself that yes, this was just as it should be.

On August 2nd she landed in Singapore after the long, overnight flight from Sydney. The air outside the airport was so thick and wet after the canned gas of the airplane that she struggled with her first few breaths of it. Her squeaky-clean, thoroughly air-conditioned taxi deposited her at the Hotel Rendezvous, a mid-size establishment with a rounded, British colonial façade. It wasn't Raffles, but it wasn't The Holiday Inn either. The lobby was cool and dark until her eyes adjusted to the low light. The ceilings were low as well, which made Judith think that, while foresighted in many ways, British architects hadn't imagined just how large human beings would grow in the 20th century.

Once she was checked in, a bellboy took her suitcase, and she headed for the breakfast buffet, a riot of sliced mango, papaya, rock melon, dragonfruit, pineapple and watermelon, fried noodles with limes, and stainless steel chafing dishes of sausages, pancakes, and baked beans. She registered as she sat down at a small table by the window that she was about to eat her first meal alone in a hotel in her life. She watched quite a few other solitary eaters around her, and let them watch her.

The room she could afford was small, but the bed was large and simply made. In order to accommodate it, the bedside tables, the armchair, the desk and the bathroom were all small. But darling, Judith decided. It was a room for sleeping in, that was clear. She took a nap.

Waking at nearly eleven, Judith used the toilet, thinking it was funny how the first bowel movement in a new country deposited the remains of food from the previous one. She had a thorough shower which made her feel she had rubbed Sydney off and had really arrived in Singapore. She dressed, took a deep breath and a long, long look at herself in the bathroom mirror. The way her heavy, strawberry blond hair had been newly cut still looked a bit raw, but she liked the way her new lipstick seemed to diminish her jowls. She dug her sunglasses out of her suitcase, picked up her handbag, and went back downstairs. Turning left out of the hotel, she walked to the Singapore Art Museum, also a colonial building, formerly a boys' school. Inside, she spent less time studying the art on the walls than she did imagining the rooms full of Chinese boys in long tunics with long plaits down their backs. Returning outside, she retraced her steps, turned the corner, and walked toward Little India.

She had visited with Bill and the kids on their way to Bintan. Then, they had concentrated on the wares— bangles for Claudia, incense and knock-off watches for the boys, embroidered cushion covers for the living room. This time, she couldn't take her eyes off the faces, the generous gleaming hair and potential drama in the eyes of the young men, the nose jewelry and rocking gait of the old women. She knew that the red dot in the middle of the forehead meant that a woman was married, but she wanted to know what marks they carried if they were widowed.

No one in the throng reminded her of Danesh Rupani. She remembered his light brown skin looking dry. She had a vague recollection of clinging to him for a moment when he arrived on Bintan after Bill's disappearance, when she had been shocked and salty and sticky, but had noticed his very pleasant cologne. The men in Little India gleamed like manuka honey and smelled of everything but posh perfume.

Elsewhere in the city, other tourists were visiting the spiceless shopping centers along Orchard Road. Judith told herself she'd have a look around in the shops the next day, if she felt the interview went well. Truth be known, she'd also go to the shops if it went badly. She was much too big for almost all Singapore fashions, but the shoes seemed to fit her.

Returning to her room from dinner that evening she castigated herself for eating too much again. Her stomach was beginning to churn. How was she going to get the sleep she needed? Switching on the lights she saw that her bed had been turned down, and a fresh orchid bloom lay on her pillow. After changing into her cotton nightie and lighting the vanilla-scented candle her therapist had recommended she bring along ("Just think about the flame, Judith. Just think about the flame."), Judith slept for twelve hours straight.

"Good morning, Mrs. Reynolds. I'm glad to see you again under these far better circumstances." Danesh Rupani pulled out one of the chairs for her in front of his desk and sat down opposite her in another. The carpet was royal blue and the walls white, the same colors as the waiting room and all the Club Med advertising Judith had ever seen. The sun beat on the window and the glass must have been getting quite hot, but the air in the room was obliviously cool.

"Well, I must say," said Judith, conscious that her upper lip was wet and her mouth was dry, "it's funny, but it feels good to be back."

"Good flight?"

"Can't complain. And the hotel's lovely." He looked so relaxed. She folded her hands in just the way he was doing and found it relaxed her as well. "You've got a nice office," she said.

The senior vice president smiled and cleared his throat. "I think you can imagine that Club Med might consider hiring you as a great risk."

Judith, although surprised that the small talk was already over, had anticipated this. "I understand."

He smiled again and gave her an appreciative nod with his sleek head. Then he raised his hands and gestured as if he were pushing something toward her. "Imagine with me, if you will. You arrive. You settle into your job. The guests come and go, so perhaps you feel no need to confide in them. But there's a colleague you like. Maybe someone in the Petit Club. Maybe another Australian. You're in the habit of taking your breakfast together. Or you share a day off. You feel comfortable. How do you avoid speaking about your husband's death?"

Judith pressed her lips together. "I won't mention the drowning."

"You're sure you want to keep it a secret?"

"Yes."

He looked surprised. "Why?"

"I should think it was obvious, Mr. Rupani." She meant this to come out simply, but she felt herself tipping her head forward a little, looking at him through her eyelashes.

"What should be obvious?"

Judith straightened her head up and spread her hands so he'd know she wasn't conniving. "That I want to do exactly what you want me to do," she said.

Danesh inclined his head again. "Much obliged," he said, "but I believe we all need someone to talk to, Mrs. Reynolds."

"Oh, please call me Judith," she giggled. "You make me feel older than I really am."

"All right," he smiled, and let his comment about confidences hang in the air, gazing levelly at her.

She took a moment to think. This was a test. Why did he seem to be enjoying it? Her last few answers had clicked into place. She wondered if a lie would be riskier than the truth and then answered him honestly. "I already have a therapist, Mr. Rupani. I don't need another one."

She watched him exhale, as if he had been holding his breath. His face cleared and he said, "There we are, then."

Judith installed her daughter in boarding school, gave

the Volvo to her older son, sold the Audi, and arrived on Bintan on December 11th in the middle of an influx of a whole new set of employees. Training in Australia had been rigorous and interesting. Some people called it indoctrination, but Judith didn't mind it a bit. Initially hyper-conscious of the age difference, in the second week she felt some of the young people gather around her when she found the courage to offer an opinion or anecdote. Her eight-year-olds had surrounded her similarly when she took them to Sydney's Museum of Natural History and told them about the early humans.

It rained for the thirty-six hours she spent in Singapore, but on Bintan, only forty-five minutes south by ferry, it was bright. Fast-moving clouds raced for the sun, then left it behind, much like on the day she and her family had arrived nearly a year before. During the ride on the Club Med bus from the ferry terminal to the resort, Judith remembered how they had all felt depressed by the island scenery. There was simply nothing of interest to look at along the road. The Indonesian government had designated the island for the development of resorts, and that's all there were, ringing the coast and invisible to anyone but paying guests. This time, though, she didn't feel depressed when she looked out the window. She felt electrified by a sense of dutiful, if morbid, curiosity. Arriving at Reception and waiting with the others to receive her room key, she told no one how much she wanted to go straight down to the beach and walk right into the water, stepping carefully.

She and the two other women who had arrived on the same ferry were shown to their rooms. Both of the others—a twenty-year-old Australian who had been trained at Club Med in Bali to teach in the circus school and a twenty-six-year-old Japanese who had spent the last year in the Maldives—made Judith feel like a bit of a hippo, but the Japanese girl's bad skin was a consolation.

The resort's main building sat at the top of the slope with a somewhat charmless authority, its two perpendicular wings embracing the pools and indicating the direction of the trapeze, the trampoline, and the beach. Beyond the right wing were the uncompromisingly rectangular guestroom buildings, and beyond the left wing were the staff quarters. In between there were paths of brick and paths of sand, and bougainvillea after bougainvillea after bougainvillea.

They'd meet the village chief at lunchtime, which gave them about half an hour to unpack. Judith put her new evening wear (Club Med had recommended that she have at least two cocktail dresses and a gown suitable for tropical weather) in the narrow closet and filled her drawers with the regulation uniforms—polo shirts and Bermuda shorts. Her old panties looked faded and weary by comparison. Perhaps, on her first day off, she'd go back to Singapore for new ones. But they wouldn't fit, would they? She heard the Australian trapeze artist, Jack, getting acquainted with the bathroom they would share. Judith joined her and they each chose a drawer. Over time, they would come to share Judith's hair dryer, which was more powerful than Jack's was, and Jack's much more effective tweezers.

Abdel, the village chief, was handsome and well built, and had a beautiful voice. During their lunch in the main buffet restaurant (Judith resisted getting up for thirds) she imagined him kissing her. Her heart stopped. She felt ridiculous. How long had she been staring? Had people been trying to talk to her? Surely he had understood the look on her face. Trying to recover, she felt ridiculous again. Her eyelashes fluttered like butterflies trying to land in a stiff wind.

At home, Judith had risen early, making herself a cup of tea or instant coffee and drinking it on the back porch, listening to the kookaburras high up and invisible in the trees. At Club Med she got up at six to walk up and down the beach. Being so close to the equator meant twelve hours of sun, every day, all year. At six, the sky wasn't yet light, but was thinking about it. Bintan's beaches were challenging, with bays formed by eruptions of dark gray rock. The trees that found purchase among them grew outwards rather than up, with gray branches twisting and looping toward the light. Once the sun was up, the kingfishers they hid would start screaming, but at six they slept. By nine the beach would be swept clean by the quiet local men who were bused in for the job, but at this early hour the rough water's broken and twisted offerings lay in a swath several feet wide. Judith perused it slowly. There was enough light to distinguish bones by.

She and Jack had quickly developed a code. If Jack left her door to the bathroom slightly open it meant she wanted Judith to wake her when she returned from her morning walk. If the door was closed, Jack had to get her own tight little bottom out of bed. The open door reminded Judith of her daughter and how welcoming she used to be when Judith went in to wake her each day. The closed door had the same grim look as the doors to her boys' bedrooms.

When she let herself in one morning halfway through her second week on the island, the phone was ringing.

"Hello?"

"Mum?"

"Claudia! Hello, my girl! How are you?"

"I'm fine. How about you?"

"I'm fine. I think I'm pretty good. Just got back from a walk on the beach. Going to have a shower, head up to the restaurant . . ."

Claudia cut in. "What about Dad, Mum?"

"Dad?" For a crazy moment Judith wondered if Claudia had chosen to forget that he had drowned.

"Of course Dad. I thought you were looking for Dad."

"I was, darling. I am. I was walking on the beach looking for him just now. Like I do every morning. It's not the only thing I'm doing, though. And actually, I'm doing my best not to talk about him while I'm here."

"I'd think you could probably make an exception for me, Mum." Claudia's voice was clipped. Judith reminded herself that her daughter was thirteen.

"Of course you're right, sweetie. Don't imagine that I wouldn't tell you, though."

"Okay."

Judith took a chance. "Would you want to come to Bintan if Dad's bones turned up?"

She let her daughter think.

Claudia said, "I want a plot in a cemetery and I want his bones to be buried there. But I don't want to see them."

"Fair enough, darling," Judith said warmly, and then, more brightly, "Tell me more about you."

"Like what?"

Judith took her daughter's sullenness in stride. It never occurred to her that Claudia might be trying to hurt her. "Well, how are your classes going? Still enjoying the Spanish?"

"Yeah. It's good. Maybe I'll do a year abroad or something."

Judith took this at face value as well. "Get away for bit. That'd probably be good."

"Maybe. I've got to get going, Mum."

"Already? Well, I love you, my girl. Take good care. God bless."

"Love you, too. Bye."

It sounded like loveyoutoobye.


Danesh Rupani came over for the party on New Year's Eve. He wasn't obvious at dinner, but Judith saw him later, standing by the stage that had been constructed by the pool. She stayed with a couple of the families of her Petit Club kids during the eternity of lip synching, and then there was the overlong, overblown "presentation of the cocktails." With two glasses of champagne inside her—it had been Jack's idea to celebrate while they were dressing themselves—Judith was completely charmed. The cocktails were beautiful—three varieties of drinks in three different colors, topped not with little umbrellas but with local flowers and bits of carved fruit. While the adults obediently watched the spectacle being staged in and around the pool, the children sidled up to the tables and fondled the stems of the glasses, then the blooms. A few dared to stick in a finger and taste the drink. Judith didn't interfere.

Danesh stood to one side, straight-backed, wearing a half smile. Judith made her way over.

"Isn't it lovely?" she beamed.

"Yes," he replied, speaking to her bosom.

She lost him when the crowd turned around and fell on

the drinks. Then there was the conga line Judith helped lead through the main building and into the disco. Each member of the staff had a schedule for the night, either to dance with the guests and then take a clean-up shift or to clean up and then dance. Judith could dance until 1:30, and then she had to go back outside to pick up trash while others dismantled the stage.

She had been dancing for about half an hour—mostly with a group of five young Japanese women who sat down when she went to get a drink of water and stood up again when she returned—when she noticed Danesh standing nearby, just off the dance floor. Her dancing style hadn't seemed important with the guests; now it suddenly did. But she couldn't just stop. She also couldn't just improve. Anyway he was smiling at her, so maybe it was okay to carry on as she was. It was a little disconcerting that he remained immobile as she boogied over. Maybe he wasn't a dancer. Bill certainly hadn't been.

When she reached Danesh the music changed, slowed down, which concerned her further, as she only felt comfortable with jiggly little steps. Noting her confusion, he took his hands out of his pockets and reached one out toward her. She watched it land on her chest, his palm on her cleavage, feeling her heart, his long middle finger at the base of her throat, feeling her pulse. Gently he pushed her backwards onto the dance floor, took his hand from her skin and slid it around into the small of her back. Judith surprised herself by not stepping on his toes as he did so.

"Just sway," he said directly into her ear, causing her to shiver.

She tried. "What do I do with my hands?" she shouted.

She couldn't hear it when he laughed, but it was lovely to watch. "Whatever you like," he enunciated.

She left her hands down by her sides.

Danesh raised his eyebrows. "I see," he said. She read his lips. He started to say something else, then stopped himself. She had felt his hand flatten a bit harder into her back, then relax again.

"What?" she mouthed.

His face broadcast a decision made. "Do you still want to do exactly what I want you to do?" he asked.

Judith felt drunk again, although she was sure she had sweated all the champagne out during the conga. "I think so," she said.

He nodded. "Then hold my lapels."

She did. It was as if her legs had ceased to exist, and his were sufficient for both of them.

He was smiling at a few of the guests, and she twisted her wrist and peeked at her watch. There was time for one more dance, and she prayed for another slow one. The pace changed slightly. Danesh nodded his head to show her the beat. Imitating him, perhaps a little too enthusiastically, she dislodged the combs that held her hair off her face. He used his free hand to catch them before they fell on the floor. "Ill keep them for you," he said in her ear, slipping them into his pocket.

After clean-up, Judith wanted to look for Danesh, but she didn't want it to be too obvious. She gave up after explaining to a few of the staff that he had her combs and maybe he was leaving and had they seen him? He couldn't have gone far, but she couldn't bring herself to hunt for him. She couldn't go back to her room yet, either. Taking off her sandals, she walked down to the beach, out of reach of the festive lights. Looking at the black ocean, she shivered as she realized that Bill was somewhere in front of her and Danesh was somewhere behind her. It seemed as if it should be the other way around.

Leaving her room the following morning, she trod on her combs. Ruining them became unimportant when she realized that Danesh must have left them there on the floor for her. Perhaps he had stood outside her room for a moment while she slept. Perhaps he had put his ear to the door.

There were days now when Bill didn't cross her mind on these walks. When she realized this, usually walking back to her room to wake up Jack, she would hurry back down to the beach and feel vaguely guilty casting her eyes along the edge of the water for her husband's remains. On January

27th, Judith woke unusually early and found herself on the beach at five-thirty. The waves didn't roar as loud now that the monsoons had passed, and the water on her left as she marched along the sand was a more companionable presence than it had been in December. She remembered to think about Bill's bones, and her thoughts traveled back from the end to the beginning of their life together.

On the day Bill had proposed marriage, she had asked him not to come over, as she wasn't feeling well. It turned out she had the mumps. Already, on their date two evenings before, she had been running a fever. Bill had mistaken her glittering eyes and flushed face for enthusiasm and had started talking about his plans for their future. When she lowered her eyes and pushed the food around on her plate, he imagined that her stomach was full of butterflies of delight. She was silent as he drove her home, but her lips, when he kissed her at the door, were like fire.

She told him she wasn't well two days later, but he showed up at her parents' front door at 11:30 a.m., wearing a double-breasted suit and carrying an enormous bunch of roses in his tough young hands. Standing on the doorstep, Judith felt dizzy in the sunlight. Bill didn't appear to notice her swollen face, her bathrobe, her unkempt hair. She realized he was talking, and the lines on his forehead told her that he was asking her something. "Will you? Will you?" he said, over and over. Judith took a deep and difficult breath. Inhaling, she thought that this was not what she had imagined, indeed it was rather what she had been dreading. Exhaling, she thought of poor Bill brushing his still-wet hair into place, buttoning his shirt, buying flowers, thinking only of her and their future together on the drive to her house. She imagined herself upstairs, asleep, and her desire for her own bed was so great she nearly fainted. Maybe she could count on Bill to have enough energy for them both. "Yes," she said, "I will," and then closed the door.

Judith found that she had stopped walking. What if Bill had proposed the week before, when she had felt fine, or a few weeks later, when she had recovered? What would she have said if his timing had been different? One of the night's last stars caught her eye and she turned toward it, facing the ocean. "Bill?" she said out loud. She was grateful when the sky lightened and the morning's first hooting birds brought her back to her senses.

There was a week in the middle of February when all of the children in her charge were boys. They loved the big climbing frame shaped like a pirate ship in the play area behind the Petit Club, and she had the feeling a few of them were just marking time during their other activities until they could get back there. She took them over to the circus school near the swimming pool, and they liked the trampoline a little, but when introduced to the trapeze, they thought the ladder and wires looked like rigging.

Before Judith or anyone else could stop them, they were swinging on it shouting "Aar!" at each other. By the end of Tuesday it was clear to her from experience that she would have to rewrite the basic plan for this group. If they were to have a good time on this holiday, there would have to be more than the usual menu of swimming, tennis, and storytelling.

Two little boys—Max from London, covered in freckles, and Sebastian from Amsterdam, with sand-colored bristles for eyelashes—were particularly keen. When their parents had signed them in on Wednesday morning she was ready. "Right, mates," she said, once their hats and sunblock had been stowed away, "it's time for us to get serious." They stared at her. Both had been to Club Med before, and this seemed like something new.

"How?" asked Max, and Judith could see by the working of his forehead that he was already imagining a number of things himself.

"You tell me. What do serious pirates do?"

"They attack ships?" he suggested uncertainly.

"They kill people," declared Sebastian.

"I reckon they do," said Judith. "What else? What do they wear?"

Max knew this one. "Stripy shirts! And black things over their eyes. One eye, I mean."

"And parrots," added Sebastian. "And they drink rum."

Judith laughed. "Shall we do that?"

"NO!" shouted the boys.

"What else do they do, then?" Three more boys trailed in after their breakfast, one from Switzerland with a milk moustache, one from Australia with egg, and one well-scrubbed and silent Korean. "Morning, mates!" she said broadly. "We're talking about what pirates do." She counted on her fingers: "They attack ships, kill people, wear parrots and drink rum. What else?"

That seemed to be it from the boys for the moment.

"What if a pirate ship has attacked another ship loaded with gold and jewels and guns, and it steals them all? They're worried about another pirate ship stealing their booty now, aren't they?" Nods all around. "So what do they do with it?"

"Take it home?" said the milk moustache.

"Not yet," said Judith with a twinkle in her eye. "Until they're ready to go home, what do they do with it?"

"They put it in the ground," said Sebastian.

"That's called burying," Max told him sagely.

"Right," said Judith to them both.

"And they draw a map!" piped up egg-face.

"Right again!" said Judith, about to tell them that was precisely what they would be doing today. But the boys hadn't finished embellishing the idea.

"Then they hide the map too!" said one.

"And they put a curse on the treasure," said another.

Then freckled Max raised his hands in the air and shouted, "And they leave a skeleton in the sand to frighten people off!"

A couple of the little boys started jumping. "Yeah! Yeah!" they cheered. But Judith didn't hear them. Instead, she heard the ocean, saw it grab the shore with a frothy leer and recede.

"Hmm. Are you sure about that, Max?"

"Hey. I thought you knew about pirates," he said.

"I do," she said.

"Then how come you don't know about the skeletons?"

"Skeletons," said the Korean boy, practicing the word.

"I do know," Judith insisted. "There are skeletons on all desert islands," she said, stalling.

"Is this a desert island?" asked Sebastian.

"If we say it is, mates, then it is." She bent down to their level and continued, looking into all their eyes in turn, hushed and conspiratorial. "And I know for a fact that a man was tragically drowned here, and that his bones toss in the surf each day, and that his tortured soul howls in the wind each night."

Five little wet mouths hung open.

"Why?" asked Max.

Judith stood up again.

"Because he wasn't very nice."

Silence.

"Are you afraid?" she asked.

"No," said the Korean boy.

Judith's map was a marvel. While her Japanese assistant, Miku, took the boys to the tennis courts for a while, Judith ran over to the kitchen in search of some sort of paper. No one stopped her or even looked at her questioningly, although only a few of them actually recognized her. This, and the fact that she found exactly what she was looking for—a large square of brown paper, lately wrapped around three huge wheels of Reblochon cheese—seemed to her to bestow a superior chop of approval on her project. She left the kitchen with a face flushed full of righteous blood.

Not a smoker herself, she stopped off at Reception for a lighter to burn the edges of the map before returning to the Petit Club. She didn't draw the beach. If it were too easily recognizable, the boys would run right there. She sketched a steaming cauldron (the restaurant), a waterfall (the fountain behind the swimming pool), monkeys on a thatched roof (the beach café), and, finally, in the bottom right corner of the map, a few stylized bones, a fish, and some rocks.

She knew the boys were clever enough to follow the map to the beach this afternoon, but the bone hunt could last another day at least. If they didn't find any bones by the next afternoon, she'd have something hidden to lead them to. She rolled up the map, went outside, and hid it in the pirate ship.

Turning around to head back inside, she saw Danesh Rupani peering in the window of her Petit Club room. Seeing him more or less on her turf gave her a jolt. "Danesh!" she said, without realizing she had dropped the "Mr. Rupani." He wheeled around, surprised, and put his hands in his pockets—as if to steady himself, Judith thought, but she didn't take the time to imagine why. "What brings you here?" she asked cheerily as she approached.

"I wanted to see you in action," he replied.

If Bill had said this to her, he would have looked somewhere off to the side as he did so. Danesh looked her right in her face, and it was her own eyes that skittered away. She giggled. "If you'd been looking the right way," she said, gesturing, "you'd have spotted me in action on the pirate ship."

He smiled.

"I was hiding a treasure map."

He raised his eyebrows in a question, and she noticed that they weren't heavy, but soft.

"It's all boys this week," she told him. "They're not very interested in being lions and tigers in the circus show, but they're crazy about pirates. So I'm going to give them all scars and a bit of five o'clock shadow, and they're going to hunt for buried treasure."

"Your idea?"

"Guilty," she replied with her hands held up.

He rocked back on his heels in admiration, but didn't say anything right away.

"How long are you staying this time?" Judith asked, knowing her boys must be on their way back.

"Until Friday or Saturday."

She nodded.

"Tomorrow's Valentine's Day," he said.

"Oh, my goodness, is it?" Judith laughed nervously. "Well, it's not so surprising that I overlooked it, I suppose."

"Would you like to have dinner with me?"

Her mouth fell open and she had no idea how to make it speak for her. Just then her boys came barreling around the corner. "Where is it?!" shouted Max at the head of the pack.

Judith changed gears with a deep breath and replied, "Okay. What did you lot sail over to this island on?"

"The ferry?" one offered hesitantly.

"Pirates on a ferry?" Judith guffawed, and Danesh laughed along with her.

"The pirate ship!" yelled Sebastian, and all the boys went running to start the search.

Judith switched back to Danesh. "Well, I usually eat with the kids, you see. And then I've got to change." She let her answer hang. Her heart was banging. "I'm sorry I'm so awkward at this. I haven't been invited on a date in over two decades."

Danesh waited a moment. When Judith said nothing else he prompted gently, "That wasn't an answer."

"No, I suppose it wasn't."

"You're still looking for your husband."

She shrugged. "Perhaps less than I should be."

He nodded, but he didn't look at all hurt or embarrassed. Instead he looked at her carefully and smiled. She had to wonder what he thought he was seeing.

When Danesh had gone, Judith watched the boys swarming over the ship. All the little white boys were shouting, looking fevered, passing by the map again and again without seeing it, getting frustrated. Only the silent Korean worked methodically, stumping the others by slipping the map from its hiding place and holding it quietly until they had all noticed.

At dinner that night, Abdel, the village chief, came over to the Petit Club tables. Judith remembered wanting his lips and his attention on her first day. He leaned over to talk to the boys with one hand on the table, one on Judith's shoulder. "Oh!" she thought to herself as she felt him pretending he wasn't touching her by teasing the children. Danesh wouldn't do this, she thought, and suddenly regretted having rejected his dinner invitation. Danesh, she felt very clearly, wouldn't pretend anything.

She called his room that night with her heart in her

throat, and stammered to him that she'd love to have dinner together tomorrow. He said he was delighted, sounding interested, amused.

When the boys were assembled at the Petit Club the next morning, Judith had Miku take them on a trek along the edge of the golf course, looking for the monkeys who lived there, so that she could get some treasure together.

After buying a shell-encrusted box in the boutique, she went along to the little theater, through the changing room, and into the costume master's sewing room. When she turned on the light she was momentarily distracted by sequins before going straight for the long strings of fake pearls and gold chain hanging out of a set of plastic drawers. Coiled in the box she had bought, they didn't look like much. The only precious metal she owned was her wedding band, the only jewels were the sapphire chips she'd worn in her ears since her mother died.

Judith worked up a sweat trying to get the wedding band off her finger, and when she succeeded she tried not to think. She nonetheless registered a ticklish feeling between her ribs. It wasn't glee, she knew, but it wasn't regret either. She took off the earrings as well, but they looked sad and lost and in danger of disappearing into the pile of fake pearls, so she put them back on. The ring, however, looked just right. She closed the box and took it to the beach.

No one seemed to be watching her. She walked beyond the sunbathers, beyond a clutch of rocks, and knelt in the strip of wet sand between the water and the white, powdery sand it would soon be too bright to look at. Judith didn't know much about tides, but this one appeared to have turned. She dug in the sand with her hands, watching as the water in the hole pulled it back in upon itself. The more she dug, the wetter the hole became, the more difficult to imagine fitting a box neatly inside and digging it up again. She sat back on her haunches and looked out at the surf. Suddenly she knew that Bill's bones wouldn't rise again. They were too heavy, the sand too greedy. Sometimes, she remembered, Bill would fall asleep on top of her, and she would lie awake thinking about his body. She knew, as everyone knew, that muscle was denser than fat, and weighed more. Bill had plenty of both. This was where his heft came from. But usually she couldn't get beyond the feeling that his bones were actually the heaviest things about him. His heels were like lead in the morning as he thudded to the bathroom. His thighs, when he sat, were like a concrete foundation waiting for a house. His skull was indestructible. And his phalanges, bones which looked so heartbreakingly delicate on the life-sized skeleton hanging in the corner of her classroom in Sydney, were an iron fist at rest.

The boys had spotted seven monkeys on their trek and

were optimistic about their prospects for the treasure hunt. Judith made them wait until after lunch, drew scars and stubble back on their faces, and winced when Sebastian shouted, "Aar! Time for the bone hunt!" The boys insisted on following the treasure map from the restaurant to the beach a second time and then were intent on paddling through the water, digging in with their feet, stopping to investigate when they felt something. Finally they reached the rocks and the pieces of pale driftwood she had lain one across another as a marker. The boys pulled their plastic shovels from their waistbands like swords, and dug. Her wedding ring was lost in the ensuing mess, but they divided up the other spoils by pulling them in a tug of war and then went running to their parents.

This was not what Judith was thinking about as she showered that evening. She was remembering a morning, years before, when she was making her coffee before going out to drink it on the porch. Through the screen door she watched a huge, shameless crow feeding noisily at her bird feeder. Beneath the feeder was a little female Silvereye, eating the seeds the crow sprayed down every time he changed position. The crow hopped to the porch railing, and in doing so dislodged the feeder, which fell straight down onto the little bird. The bird flopped twice, open-winged, then lay still. Aghast, Judith turned off the fire under the kettle and stepped outside, shooing the crow, which was now feeding right next to the poor

Silvereye's dead body.

Judith knew this bird. She and her mate had been busily building a nest in a tall eucalypt in her garden. She took the nearly weightless body and lay it in the thick leaves near the foot of the tree. When she came home from work in the afternoon, she heard the male Silvereye calling for his girl, and wished with a lump in her throat that she could explain to him what had happened.

Now, as she dressed on this Valentine's Day, she felt again the same cold, oily sensation in her chest that she had experienced listening to the bird's constant, unhappy song. But as she blew her hair dry and brushed it into submission, she had the inkling of a new thought. All along she had imagined that little bird calling for his mate, hour after hour, day after day. But maybe he wasn't calling for his girl. Maybe he was calling for any girl. Any girl at all.

She was smiling to herself when she came along the veranda to the Italian restaurant. Danesh wasn't, though. He looked even more recently groomed than usual, and his cream-colored jacket fit him perfectly. But when she was close enough to smell his scent there were lines between his eyebrows she had never seen before.

"You look beautiful," he said, still not smiling.

"What's wrong?" she blurted.

He said nothing.

"Tell me now, Danesh." He took a breath in through his nose and expelled it through his mouth.

Danesh looked at his feet, then at hers, up her legs, across her stomach, over her breasts, from her neck to her chin to her eyes. "I've had a complaint," he said.

"Someone objects to our eating together?" she asked.

He shook his head. "Maybe we could go to the office."

"That bad?"

"We'll see," he said, raising an arm in the direction they should go. "Shall we?"

"No," she said, a screaming between her ears. This was too much like childhood, too much like being singled out among her siblings for criticism. Too much like Bill and his violent disappointment sessions. "No. Let's walk somewhere. Tell me what's happened while we walk."

They walked in silent alarm, side by side, past Reception, down the long set of stairs, along the path leading to the guestrooms. Judith listened to the companionable sound of their evening shoes on the stairs and felt like crying. "So?" she prompted.

Danesh was staring straight ahead, as if to bore a hole through the distant jungle with his eyes. "You had the Petit Club search for bones?"

Judith stopped in her tracks and began to wring her hands. "Well, yes. And no! I mean, the boys, I mean, we all had this idea that pirates put skeletons near buried treasure to scare people away, so I told them, I mean—"

Danesh looked at her now. "What did you tell them?"

Judith dropped her hands. "I told them a dead man's bones tossed in the surf."

He nodded, then looked back at the jungle.

"It was a game, Danesh. What's happened?"

"They believed you."

"So?"

"One of them told his parents."

"So?"

"The parents asked the head of the Petit Club about it."

"So?" Judith was getting hot. This was taking too long.

"She told them your husband drowned here."

"What? How did she know?"

"I don't know."

Judith looked at the jungle now. "Are you going to have this little talk with her as well as with me?"

"Not this one."

"Why not?"

"I don't care what happens to her."

Judith thought for a moment, than started walking again, while Danesh kept pace.

"So what's going to happen to me?"

"I don't know yet. The boy's parents don't have a sense of humor. They're lodging a formal complaint, saying you are too morbid to care for children. They're spreading the word."

Judith looked back at the warm lights of the main building and imagined she could hear the buzz going around about her. She turned away again, kept walking. "What should I do, Danesh?"

He didn't say anything.

"What should you do, Danesh?"

He stopped, shrugging. "There's no training for this situation."

"Isn't it the usual?" Judith said.

"What's the usual?"

"Isn't the customer king?"

"I see. Maybe. But maybe not. I can say that the boy misunderstood."

"And the head of the Petit Club?"

"She wasn't here for the drowning. I can say she was mistaken as well."

"But people are talking. That's where the damage is."

"Judith. Are you trying to talk yourself out of a job?"

"I'm trying to help you."

Judith watched a wince pinch his face, a slight caving of his chest. Then he looked slowly up at the windows around them. Slowly he looked back down at her. Slowly he lifted his long fingers to her face and kissed her, pushing his fingers back into her hair and gripping her there. Then he put his hands back down by his sides.

"You want to help me," he said.

"Yes." It was as simple as that.

In the morning Judith was starving. The night before, she had had no dinner, had watched in astonishment as Danesh kept his eyes open and staring at her for the entire time his head was between her legs, and had experienced the first orgasm of her life. It came as a complete surprise—a speeding car on a deserted road in the dead of night.

Danesh got up first. After showering and dressing, he kissed her and opened the door. "Danesh!" she said, trying not to shout, her heart beating wildly. He came back and sat on the bed. "You're not going to drown yourself, are you?"

"No, I'm not," he answered seriously.

She nodded. "Okay, then."

He got up.

"One more thing," she said.

He sat down.

"Am I going to have to choose between you and my job?"

He took her hand and traced her soft knuckles with the tips of two fingers. "Possibly," he said. He touched her chin and brushed some hair from her forehead. He pulled the sheet down and lay his hand again on her heart, then took it away and neatly replaced the sheet. "I love your skin," he said. "Milk for my coffee."

Later that morning, after Judith had sneaked back to her own room in her evening dress to shower and change, she charged the breakfast buffet like a bull. A few heads whipped around and a few fingers pointed as she dithered over her pastry choices and had trouble fitting a deep bowl of Frosties on her tray. The apple she knew she should eat kept threatening to roll off. She knew she was blushing, but steadied herself and marched firmly over to the table where the Korean boy sat with his family. The child smiled as he saw her coming, and nodded to a seat by his mother. It was clear that he at least would be coming to the Petit Club today.

# My Thing

"My penis is a superhero," Raphael said as I crossed the living room to put away the laundry. He was sitting sprawled on the couch in his way. A lazy way. A powerful, lazy way. Like a tiger. We're successful Indian immigrants. But he's also part jungle cat.

Then the door bell rang, and it was the people from my church. We said our happy hellos, and I closed the door behind them. I led them into the living room and Raphael was gone. They couldn't see him, but I could still sense him. He was out on the terrace behind the palm tree. I showed the church people to the sofa and heard him light some incense. Then I could smell him.

I sat in the little straight-backed chair with my back to the terrace, and light was on the church people's pinched faces. I'd been hoping to have them over for so long. I thought it would help me to feel stronger and happier in my home if they left some traces on it. In the morning, I'd be able to drink out of the teacups they had used while Raphael sat opposite me with his black coffee. "Cuts right through the butter, Marina. Have a cup," he'd say, and I'd say, "No, thanks," with a smile rather than a frown for once.

But now here they were on my couch, and *they* were frowning.

"How can you bear it, Marina?" they asked.

"Bear what?" I said, knowing they meant the paintings.

"The paintings," they said.

"Oh, the paintings?" I said, looking innocently around me, eyebrows halfway up my forehead.

Raphael had started his collection when business took him to Bali and kept him there, on and off, for two years. The paintings are huge. Above the TV, just to the left of the church people, was the one of an elaborate Balinese sword on a dark background, hanging straight up and down as if suspended by some kind of force field.

"How can you live with this every day?" they asked, pointing but not looking at the sword.

"The sword? Well, that, I always try to see it as a sort of cross."

The church people sucked in their breath and averted their faces, as if I'd just sprayed them with insecticide. Behind me Raphael did his wheezy laugh, curling the hairs on the back of my neck.

The church people looked at each other.

"I think you'd better let us see them all," they said.

The painting in the hallway was of a Japanese lady in a kimono. There are no windows lighting the hall, and I was trying to glide on by, but the church people stopped.

"Is there a light, Marina?" they asked.

I flipped it on, like a guilty child, and the Japanese lady stepped right out of her picture, like she always did. Usually I kept that light off and passed her like a stranger in the street. She loved to step out of the picture, though. At least that's what Raphael said. Once, he said, she came down off the wall in the night in Bali and got into his bed. He said he told her to go back to her picture. He said.

"Do you like this painting?" the church people asked me.

I was about to say something positive about her kimono in that voice I used to use with my mother when I wanted to distract her from the obvious flaws in my character—the voice I used with Raphael when he wanted to bite my neck and I wanted to get breakfast on the table. But suddenly I felt too tired.

"No," I told them.

They nodded. We proceeded to the bedroom.

On either side of my vanity mirror was a pair of paintings of Balinese ceremonial masks. In order not to feel menaced by them when I did my makeup, I thought of them as my guards, protecting me. Although Raphael and I are both Eurasian, descendants of the Portuguese who stumbled overdressed onto the beaches of Southern

75

India four hundred years ago, we're just about as black as Indians get. We've got big Portuguese names, and just a fleck of Portuguese blood. The masks are white. That's what makes them so scary to the Balinese. White and grimacing, baring huge hooked teeth and a long strip of a leather tongue, fringed and embossed with gold. Bulbous eyes rimmed in black and red. Long hair you can imagine strangling you in your sleep.

"It's not just paint, you know, Marina," they said.

"What is it, then?"

"It's evil."

"Come on," I said.

They just stared at me.

"Come on. How are we supposed to have peace in the world if we don't respect other cultures?" These were Raphael's words.

"You feel it, don't you?"

I did. I didn't know how to put it, though. My feelings were tangled in tolerant behavior like sunken treasure in seaweed. Before I could say anything, one of them noticed the portrait above the bed. The others' eyes followed, and suddenly they pushed me back out of the room. One of them snapped the light off in the hall as we passed the Japanese lady. When we reached the living room, I could tell by the scent that Raphael had crossed through and left by the front door. For all I knew, he was merely waiting in the garage for my guests to leave, but I decided not to think about it.

"Sit down," I said. "Wouldn't you like some tea?" But they shook their heads and remained standing.

"We need to leave, Marina. We can't stay here, but we want to protect you from this evil spirit. The way we can do that is to tell you that you must get rid of these paintings and pray that you will find the courage to do so."

Then they were gone. If we had had tea I would have busied myself clearing away the cups, but the house was completely in order. So I stood for a while in the living room and made myself look at the sword as a sword and not as a cross. It seemed to me that if I wanted to think of it as a cross it should be allowed, but the spell I had woven around the image was broken.

I went into the bedroom to look at the painting above the bed. It's a dark picture, chocolate and black and gold. A portrait of me. Raphael had it painted in Bali. It doesn't resemble any photo we had of me. He said he told the artist what I looked like, but I've long thought the painting looks much more like our daughter, or how she'll look when she's a bit older. I turned on the light to bring more of the painting forward and stood stock still at the end of the bed. For eighteen years I'd been living with this painting, and I'd never noticed that you could see my thing in it. Some people sleep under a crucifix or a drawing of flowers or maybe an old map or a picture of the kids. I'd been sleeping under my own thing.

Raphael is visited by devils. They fuel his imagination and delude him. He thinks he conjures them up, but he is surely their plaything. I don't believe Raphael ever had another woman in his bed in Bali, not a real one anyway. I do believe that Japanese lady climbed off the wall, unwound herself from all that embroidered silk, and made him feel unreasonably special for a night, or many nights.

Some men really want you to tell them how naughty they are, you know. It suited mine to the tips of his hairy toes that I'm a faithful, God-fearing woman. It suited him to know he'd pulled one over on his little Christian wife by hanging a portrait of her mysterious, glistening thing above the bed.

That's why his face got so tangled when I told him I'd be keeping that one. It didn't make any sense at all to him that I didn't take a knife to the canvas. He hunched his big shoulders, and his lips were hanging open, and I closed the door on his handsome, wretched, stunted self.

On either side of my vanity mirror I now have the prettiest wall sconces you'll ever see. I've woven some dried flowers around the base of them, too. But my portrait is still above my bed. My bed. It just didn't feel right to take myself down and let myself be carted away.

# Needing Ice

It wasn't a complete surprise to me when Yumi, one of my English students from the "academy" where I teach in central Tokyo, showed up on my doorstep. After a moment's hesitation (I must admit to a slight irritation—I had just set out a nice glass of milk and some cookies for myself) I realized I was needed, and invited her in. She stepped stiffly into my arms, sobbed a time or two, and stained my yellow cotton sweater with bloody snot.

"Never mind, never mind," I crooned and patted her coarse, dyed hair. Eighteen-year-old Japanese girls who appreciate the sleek black locks God gave them are hard to find. Whenever I meet one now, it takes my breath away.

Yumi was saying, "No, no," each time I said, "It's all right." I could feel the girl's stiff, padded bra against my own rather more ample bosom. "Come," I said, guiding the child toward the small, foam-filled sofa on the tatami after she had slipped out of the ridiculous clodhoppers they call shoes here. We sat, and I offered her a box of tissues. While she wiped her face I assessed my sweater. Baking soda and cold water would probably do the trick.

Yumi's nose continued to trickle blood. "Calm yourself," I told her, "and I'll get ice for you." I spoke slowly and simply, so as not to confuse her.

My kitchen is right behind the sofa. As I popped some cubes out of the tiny ice tray from my tiny freezer, I looked at the narrow shoulders on the little baby woman sitting there and realized that I had been waiting for such an outburst for weeks. You feel as if you are growing accustomed to the suppressed tension of the Japanese, but it sets the teeth on edge, it really does. I'd get to the bottom of this problem if it killed me. I wrapped the ice in a clean dishtowel and returned to the sofa.

"Okay, then, Yumi, tell me what's up."

"I told him what you say," she said.

"I see," I said. I didn't know quite what she was talking about, but chose not to press her. I didn't want her emotions to overwhelm her English.

"He hit me," she continued.

"I see," I said again. "This is your boyfriend?"

She nodded, tears brimming anew.

"How do your parents feel about this young man?"

Yumi's face crumpled. I wasn't sure whether this was due to emotional or grammatical complexity, so I tried to clarify. "He sounds like a bad boy."

Yumi shrugged, and sobbed. "But he is so ... so attractive."

Heaven preserve us. I got up to make some tea.

Japanese people don't appear to mind long silences, and for the first time I was glad for this. I nibbled my cookies while the water came to a boil. When the tea had brewed, I brought it to the sofa and sat down with resolution.

"Let me talk to him," I said.

It's not that I feel myself to be superior to the Japanese. I just can't help myself sometimes. I'm over here to teach them English, but I can't stop at that. I just can't. They're too bloody pathetic.

Pardon my French. I got that from Daddy. We used to shock poor Mum a bit, he and I. She hadn't the slightest idea what to do with me, poor Mum. I was at least half a foot taller and twice as wide. So it was Daddy who took me in hand. "Get right on it, Margaret," he'd say about how to deal with things, and he was quite right. That's the way.

When I went off to McGill in 1967, he gave me, as a congratulatory gift, a woodblock print he had brought back from a trip to Japan a few years before. He knew I had coveted it. It wasn't like the prints of kabuki actors one now sees reproduced on cushion covers and sushi bar matchboxes, mind you. It was a contemporary print with bold, flesh-colored circles on a black background, representing the big round heads of little children, tilted inquisitively, with red triangle mouths, and tiny hands raised in gentle surprise. Very modern. They smiled sweetly at me from my dormitory room wall. They seemed to find me surprising, entertaining. Maybe I was a comfort to them, so far away from Japan.

And now, thirty years later, they're here with me in Tokyo. I've brought them back. The print has yellowed a good deal, but the children look very much at home on the living-dining wall of my small, elderly apartment.

It's quaint, my apartment. The whole neighborhood is quaint. These little buildings certainly don't predate the war, but they feel as if they've been here forever, were in fact chiseled out of Tokyo bedrock. Everyone's got their wee bonsai on the stoop, which might have been bought yesterday but looks as old as granddad.

I absolutely love the mornings. I make my way briskly down the longish hill to the subway, and I find it very fetching how the neighborhood people (Japanese all, I'm proud to say; not for me the expatriate ghetto with its fancy supermarket full of imported olives and chocolates) have begun to acknowledge me with a small bow or wave. I whistle as I walk, as Daddy did, which they no doubt find amusing. I'm a conversation piece, I'd bet.

On the subway, it's a bit of a struggle to keep my spirits so high, though. I'm as polite as I was taught to be, but I'm not too shy to wake up a couple of pasty, puffy, sweaty, sleeping salarymen in their navy blue suits (shiny at the thigh) to ask for space to sit. The girls who get on as the train gets closer to the city wear deliberately sleepy expressions, but I can tell they're not tired. They're not too tired to work extensions into their hair and make absolutely sure that their low-slung trousers do not in any way match their pinafore tops. They rub their noses with badly painted fingernails. I get the feeling they think that a good manicure will make them look as if all they want is to get married, as if the hand advertised them as good housekeepers. I know, though, that marriage is all they think about.

What else is there for them on the horizon here, really? And if that's what they really want, then why prevaricate? God gives us this wonderful opportunity to take hold of our lives and make something worthwhile out of them, but we let ourselves get confused early on, and we stay that way. I mean, *they* do. These Japanese girls, they get on the train in the morning looking completely unprepared for the day, and they do so on purpose. They know they're supposed to look like they want to be taught something, so as not to offend the stunted Japanese male ego. It's such a shame they look to Japanese boys for their education when I'm right here in front of them.

You just have to get right on it, whatever it is. I'm convinced. My entire life is testimony to the fact. I've been practicing what I preach since primary school, when I started developing both physically and mentally a bit faster than the other girls. I got to the scenes of scuffles even before the teachers did. I'd listen to the recriminations at the bottom of the slide or in the sandbox, I'd give my measured judgement, and then I'd ask, "Now, does that make sense?" Invariably it did, even if someone cried over the sense it made.

There were girls who hated me for my sense, of course, when we were in high school. Their rolled-up skirts and their cigarettes made me uneasy, but I trusted God and Daddy's continuing approval, and poor Mum's constant wide-eyed surprise at herself for having produced such a strong daughter. If only I had had occasion to speak to the bad girls, to step one foot into their musky circle. I suspect they knew I'd make sense, and they felt too much peer pressure to be the first one to agree with me.

Later, when I had become a teacher, this type of girl would come to me, you know. They did. Always after school, never in a group. Their coming alone was proof positive that they really wanted advice, no matter what they actually chose to say to me. Even if they were just pretending to drop off a ragged assignment, I'd seize the opportunity to offer something back. "Take care of your wild heart," I'd say to a departing back, or "Don't take that Monique too seriously." They'd stiffen, or pretend not to have heard at all. Each time it was perfectly obvious— sometimes it even hurt me a little it was so obvious—that I had chosen my mark correctly, and had hit it.

It was with a similar sense of purpose that I tied neat bows on my brogues and set off to confront

Yumi's molester.

Kengo works in a video rental shop on a side street near the English academy where I teach and Yumi studies. Yumi wants to be a flight attendant, and she'll need to pass an English test to do so. If you ask me, she should also take a personality test, which she'd fail. It's unbelievable how these girls think they're revealing themselves with their yellow hair and their thumb rings, when in fact they're playing hide-and-please-by-no-means-seek. The little bits of themselves with which they might make a joke or dare to proffer an original idea are squirreled away in empty rooms whose keyholes and cracks are plugged up with white lipstick and rock and roll posters and Hello Kitty paraphernalia. Myself, I'd consider it beneath me even to wax off my little moustache. It would feel too much like suicide.

I wanted to bring Yumi along to meet Kengo with me, to show her how to talk sense to people, but she insisted on staying home and waiting for the outcome. I can't say I wasn't a bit relieved that she declined my invitation, however. There was no question that I knew what I'd say; it was just that I'd never confronted a young man before. Girls, middle-aged friends who drank a bit much, fathers who came in to the high school to complain about my curriculum, yes. Young men, no, never.

When I called Kengo to make our appointment, his

perfect, American-accented English took me off-guard. Yumi had explained that he had lived in the States, but I'm sure she had no conception of just how foreign he is. I was surprised, then, when the fellow who greeted me in the coffee shop with an expressionless wave looked like any other Japanese video rental employee—long hair in a ponytail, ripped black T-shirt, dull silver ear cuff. He stood out when he stood up, however. He was enormously tall.

"What can I get you?" he asked handsomely. I had expected him to be sullen.

"Oh, just coffee's fine," I said, a little brightly for my own taste. He moved off to the counter. I checked that the floor was clean before putting my bag down, and sat. I'm a bit broad for Japanese coffee shop chairs. I hoped this interview wouldn't take terribly long.

When Kengo returned and sat opposite me, I said, "Yumi didn't tell me your English was so good."

"Yumi wouldn't know good English if it bit her on the butt," he said.

"Oh dear, now, that's a bit harsh, don't you think?"

"Tell me I'm wrong," he said, looking me straight in the eye.

I couldn't. He was dead right. He understood me, and he knew it. He leaned back in his chair and spread his hands in an "I rest my case" gesture. Then with a subtle adjustment of the level of his narrow eyes—eyelids like the slightest razor nicks in a beautiful skin drum—he regarded me in my entirety. Although we weren't speaking, Yumi was no longer the subject of our conversation. *I* was. The look lasted only a second or two, but suddenly, and this has never happened to me in my life, I felt he knew the curls in my armpits, the folds in my neck, the dark of my navel, the sweat of my toes.

*Get right on it*, I thought, blocking the memory of Yumi's helpless shrug: "But he is so attractive."

"Well, it's clear you don't respect her," I said, willing ice cubes onto my prickling tongue. (It's an extraordinary sensation, the prickling tongue.)

He laughed, and our coffee arrived.

"Milk?" he inquired, and we were back to square one, he the gentleman, me nonplussed.

"What are you doing working in a video store?" I asked after he had poured for me. He took his black, with three sugars.

"It's somewhere to go."

"There are lots of places to go," I said.

"Not in Tokyo, there aren't. Not if you don't want to wear a suit."

"What about the rest of the world?"

"Who made you my guidance counselor?"

I had lost sight of my objective twice in only a few minutes. Of course I was dying to point Kengo toward employing more of his obvious intelligence. At the same time there was the issue of my prickling tongue, and ridiculously I wanted him to size me up again. But Yumi was waiting.

I had to clear my throat. The coffee shop's fake milk was cloying.

"How do you feel about hitting Yumi?"

He must have been anticipating this question, but still he made a show of stretching his body out better to consider it. I kept my feet tucked up under my chair, although doing so cut off my circulation and made me feel a bit faint. If I moved my feet forward they'd most certainly touch his.

While he was thinking, a small group of young women entered and sat down next to us. Kengo never glanced their way, though I was distracted by my desire to take a gander and categorize them for myself. But then Kengo was leaning forward to speak to me.

"Yumi's like a puppy," he said. "She's a cocker spaniel, always wanting to please, always needing to be fed. She wants to be with me, she's got to be a German shepherd."

Now this was more like it. This I could work with.

"If you hit a cocker spaniel, does it turn into a German shepherd?"

Got him. He raised his eyebrows in recognition of my acuteness, and changed his tack.

"I went like this," (here he threw his hands up in exasperation) "and she *got in the way*."

"Her nose was bleeding."

"She got in the way."

I believed him. God help me, I believed him. I forced myself to carry on, raising my eyebrows, stirring my cold coffee, cocking a pinky.

"Sounds to me like she got up your nose."

"She was talking crap."

"Oh? What was she saying?" This was perfectly arch. Perfectly.

"Something lame about the importance of trust."

My heart suddenly went tiny, the size of a cold glass marble. She had told him exactly what I had told the girls one day in class. I had grown tired of our little conversations about the weather, our clothes, our brothers and sisters. So I asked them what was important. And when I got frustrated with their answers, I *told* them what was important.

"And that's crap, is it?"

"Look at me!" he said, exasperation raising the pitch of his voice. "Do I look trustworthy?!"

I was so surprised I felt myself smile, and had to look down.

Kengo continued. "She doesn't want to be with me because she can trust me. She wants to be with me because I turn her on."

"So ..." I had to clear my throat again. "So talk of trust is premature?"

"Premature? It's insane. Not to mention hypocritical.

First she wants danger. Now she wants trust. Or she says she wants trust. My guess is she ran out of things to talk about and wanted to sound interesting."

I nearly gasped. He thought of Yumi exactly the way I did. And yet I had been so wrong about her at the same time.

"Trust isn't sexy, Margaret," he continued. "Not to girls like Yumi. It should be, but it isn't. She doesn't really want it."

I'm sure my mouth was hanging open. His use of my given name had hit me like lightning. He could have fed me lizards and I would have chewed and swallowed.

He sat back and laughed a little to himself, shaking his head, looking at the table. "Mind if I smoke?" he said, looking up.

"Yes, I do mind. I mind everything."

"What?"

"You've wasted Yumi's time." It wasn't what I really felt, but it was all I could come up with to say.

"No, I haven't," he said plainly. "I've given her exactly what she wants."

Then he raised a finger and I flinched because I thought he was going to hit me.

"Don't forget that I'm the sex object here, not Yumi, okay? *I'm* the one being objectified."

This time he might as well have hit me. I felt bruised already. And if you must know (yes, you must, I have to tell someone), I wanted to feel his fingers on my face, however it came about.

I left after that. I don't know what I said. I was exhausted. I must have mumbled something, but all I remember is wiping my lips and collecting my bag and the cool air on my burning face in the horrible narrow street I had until that moment loved.

As I walked back up the hill to my apartment, I realized that Yumi didn't deserve him. I had to decide what to say to her, because I certainly couldn't say that.

She was waiting outside my apartment, as we'd arranged, and I let us in, making a fuss over getting our coats off and putting on the kettle for tea.

"*Anno* ..." she said from the sofa in that irritating way they have of avoiding coming straight to the point. I told myself to get right on it, and sat down next to her.

"Listen to me carefully, Yumi," I said, holding her by the shoulders while she tried to hide behind her hair. "You must stay away from that boy. If he hits you once, he'll hit you again."

"Maybe not," she said.

"Oh, he will," I said, dropping my hands in disgust. "You're like a dog to him, and what do people do when dogs don't behave?"

"So how to behave? You tell me how to behave!"

"Think for yourself, young woman," I said. "Think

with your brain this time."

"I can't! Since I know him, I have no brain!" She was beginning to rock back and forth, and I could see snot glistening at the base of one nostril.

I slapped her.

I've taken down the woodblock print Daddy gave me and put it in a closet. You see, when Yumi stopped keening and looked at me in shock, I stood up and asked her to leave, to grow up a bit and pull herself together. I closed the door on her back and turned around and looked into the simple round faces of the children. Suddenly, they didn't look so innocent anymore. Suddenly they looked wicked. Worse. They looked as if they'd been laughing at me all this time.

# Being Japanese

When Sayuri was a child, her mother told her to eat all the seaweed in her soup because it would make her hair nice and black.

"What about blond people?" Sayuri asked.

"What?"

"Will it make their hair black too?"

Her mother's utter incomprehension invaded the small house, and Sayuri felt short of breath. She rinsed out her bowl and took herself outside for a walk. It was the weekend. After school on Saturdays she did homework, but on Sundays there was nothing to do. No family outings, no siblings, no pets, no cooking to help with because miso soup was so easy, and anyway her mother preferred to feed them individually wrapped bread products from the corner store.

For Sundays, Sayuri created a game in which she walked until she was lost. She'd continue in a direction, turning away from anything familiar, until she no longer recognized any landmarks, then she'd keep walking. Sooner or later she'd locate a train line and could ask directions to the closest station. She'd study the train map on the wall long enough to understand how to get home, but she'd try not to remember the name of the station she had walked to. Back in her parents' house, flushed and footsore, she treasured not knowing where she'd been all day.

When Sayuri was an adult, these solitary walks to escape the confines of her neighborhood became solitary holidays to escape the confines of the country. Still living with her parents like nearly all unmarried Japanese, she saved the money she earned teaching Japanese to wealthy expatriate businessmen, then took off. She promised herself not to speak Japanese on these trips, but at the end of each day she talked to herself in a simple journal.

From a valley in Scotland where she volunteered at a home for profoundly handicapped children:

*Marcus's head is too large. Felix's head is much too small. But it takes the same effort to pull them along the road with me. I'm so used to their weight now. When I leave, what will I do with my two hands?*

From a hut in Zambia:

*Today I met a little boy with a toy car. It wasn't a toy any Japanese child would recognize: a long piece of rusting wire curled into a steering wheel at the top, and wrapped around a stick at the bottom, with makeshift wheels on either side. After I took a photo he tore off in a cloud of dust.*

From a beachside bungalow in Venezuela, where she had traveled for once with a colleague:

*Mayuko disappears at night. I wouldn't mind, if she didn't look so confused and tired at breakfast the next day.*

From a cheap hotel in central China, off-limits to foreigners, where she convinced the clerk that she was Chinese:

*I did a terrible job of fabricating an address for myself, and I carried none of the appropriate identity cards. Maybe he believed I am simply underprivileged, even by Chinese standards. Probably a little brain-damaged as well. He seemed to consider my face honest. Some Chinese are willing to claim me for themselves.*

Sayuri felt Japanese rules of conduct like a second skeleton, which dissolved when she traveled. Abroad, it didn't seem to matter what she wore, and as a result she always knew what to put on. In Japan her clothes felt all wrong. She had a recent photo of herself, taken not long before she was bedridden. Her mother had insisted they needed a brief change of scene, and they'd traveled—leaving her father at home on the couch—to a hotel near Mount Fuji. Though longing for loose trousers and a pullover, Sayuri had dressed for dinner in a dark dress, stockings, and shoes with heels. She posed stiffly on the restaurant balcony for the photograph, holding a glass of juice, unable to smile, while Mount Fuji hummed its one constant note in the distance behind her.

There was so much you couldn't say.

Once, at her annual physical, the doctor detected lumps in her colon. His hair was carefully oiled, so it was difficult to judge its cleanliness, but his fingernails were long and gray with filth, which made it unspeakably obscene when he told Sayuri the lumps might indicate cancerous tumors. She was directed to a fancy hospital for a second opinion and had to drink barium. Several days later she was told not to worry, that they had been mistaken, there were no lumps. Two years later, at another annual physical, the doctor felt a lump in her left breast. Back at the hospital again, she had an X-ray, and although she wasn't invited to view the picture, she'd been instructed by the waxy-skinned specialist to discuss developing a work schedule that would allow for weekly chemotherapy. She and her parents met about it with the head of the language school she taught for, but then the doctor called to tell her she didn't need to undergo any treatments at all. *Why not?* She heard the question in her brain in English, then Chinese, then Spanish, but was unable to verbalize it in Japanese. You simply didn't say "Why not?" to doctors in Japan. Just like you never touched the Queen of England and never wrote someone's name in red in China. "I understand," she said.

For as long as she could remember, her father had been almost completely silent. Maybe he didn't speak much because he found his own voice as shocking as she did. While it was almost impossible for Sayuri to raise her voice, her parents had a hard time tempering theirs, as if they had to push extremely hard to talk at all. So her father didn't talk unless he was the only one available to answer the phone. Then he shouted.

At meals, Sayuri and her mother talked, and Sayuri ferried messages between her parents. She knew a message was coming when her mother pursed her big, almost perfectly circular mouth over her aggressive teeth and puckered her chin like a peach pit before erupting: "The upstairs sink is dripping."

"Is it really?" Sayuri would respond, although she'd noticed it herself. "Don't worry. Father will take care of it."

Her mother would grunt, and on the weekend the sink problem would be remedied.

Her father had begun spending his days on the couch when he retired. Her mother stood it as long as she could before going out and getting a job cleaning offices at dawn. She said it was for the money, but Sayuri knew this wasn't the case since their conditions didn't improve with the extra paycheck. They could afford to buy a hot water heater for the kitchen, but instead they continued washing the dishes in cold water, then dousing them with a kettle of hot to kill

101

germs. And rather than splurge on more frequent loads of laundry or new underwear, Sayuri continued, like her mother, to rinse her panties and stockings out in the bath with her before bed each night. Until she couldn't bathe herself.

Being Japanese was frankly exhausting. Maybe this was what was killing her. Since no one was willing to tell her exactly what was turning her yellow and sapping her strength, maybe she could decide for herself what was wrong. She could tell she was shrinking. She'd always been small, but now she was tiny. Incontinent. Skinny. Flat-chested. Why had she agonized during the second cancer scare that she was going to lose a breast? Now she had no breast to lose. At 36, she was a child again.

As preschoolers, she and the other children wore their names in small, brightly colored plastic sheaths, pinned to their clothes. At first all the names were written in *hiragana*, the phonetic Japanese script. Once they'd learned to read and write their own and everyone else's names, they moved on to elementary school and the rigors of *kanji*, Chinese characters. But Sayuri's parents did not give Sayuri a character. When all the other children's nametags switched to *kanji*, Sayuri's maintained its phonetic simplicity: sa-yu-ri. The other children teased her. "You're still in *hiragana*," they said, as if she were still in diapers. What Sayuri felt, but did not say, was that they had gone over to the Chinese while she hadn't needed to change. She knew *hiragana* was the original Japanese script, and it satisfied her.

As an adult, though, being Japanese was too hard. She studied Japanese flower arranging for seven years, but in the end felt only a superficial relationship to the teacher she'd assisted for so long. She tried to learn to play the three-stringed *shamisen*, but that teacher was grumpy and money-grubbing. Sayuri was tired of digging for her Japanese-ness and having only the shovel to show for it.

She prayed. Not to Buddha, like her mother, but to Jesus. She had never trusted Buddha. He was intelligent and peaceful, but he was too jolly. Jesus seemed to have a much better idea of the conditions people suffered.

This week it was Sayuri's family's turn to clean the garbage drop, and her father was sweeping along the edge of the three-sided enclosure with a half-size broom, pushing leaves and bottle tops into a small, long-handled dustpan. After he tipped the mess into a plastic shopping bag, he tied it at the top and brought it inside until the next garbage pick-up, two days off. He'd become very serious about garbage day since the time they'd forgotten that plastic bottles were to be recycled rather than discarded and their garbage bag had been left behind on the narrow, gray, east Tokyo street for all to see. Now he tidied the enclosure with military precision and, at the end of the week, passed the wooden baton that served as a reminder to the next family on the roster.

Sayuri heard her father come back into the house. Soon her mother would be home as well and could help her to the toilet. No doubt she'd talk about the weather. Sayuri hoped she wouldn't wet the bed again today. But then again it looked like she might. And worse. If she was going to get help, she'd have to call out now, since her father couldn't be roused once he fell asleep. "Father!" she shouted, her voice an equal mix of urgency and apology. "Father!" She heard his answering grunt. He was at her door surprisingly quickly, lifting his eyebrows and letting his mouth hang open in an unspoken question. He stopped at the threshold. "Toilet," she said.

Sayuri registered the oddity of the moment as her father crossed to her: he'd never entered her room before. There was no awkwardness in not speaking. She pushed herself onto her elbows and he pressed at her upper back until she could swing her legs over the side of the bed. He took her arms in his strong hands—she had no idea what he'd done in the first half of his life to make his hands so competent now—making her float across the floor as he propelled her toward the toilet.

"I'll wait," he said, closing the flimsy door behind her.

Sayuri felt dizzy, and suddenly her head ached. She closed her eyes and steadied herself on the wall. When the stars cleared she pulled down her pajama bottoms and sat on the seat. Strangely, although this was an old house, it had always had a Western rather than a squat toilet. She was thankful now, as she couldn't have used a squat toilet today without someone to brace her. She closed her eyes again and let go. No doubt her father heard all the farting and splashing, and Sayuri was embarrassed for him. Her belly hurt.

Depleted and wiped clean, Sayuri flushed and washed her hands. When she turned the handle she felt her father pulling the door open for her.

"That was fast," he said as he steered her back to her room. "No time to read," she answered, although she knew he wouldn't respond to this reference to his own marathon sessions in the toilet. She thanked him when she reached her bed. He stayed to see her settled.

# Tiptoe

A my embarked on her daily fifteen-minute battle
with the equatorial sun. She put on her sandals
and walked out of the cool, marble-floored apartment at
noon, rode down twelve floors in the roomy elevator, and
stepped through the sliding glass doors. For the first week
that four-year-old Elise had attended the nearby preschool,
Amy had insisted on taking her there on the back of her
bicycle. That's what she had done in Nashua; it seemed
silly to do otherwise just because they were in Singapore.
By week two they had started going by taxi.

She stepped over the legs of two sleeping gardeners,
marveling as she did every day at their ability to slip out of
their hot rubber boots and lie down on the cement, fling
an arm over their faces, and sleep. She wondered where
they came from; they were all so dark. Their language,
when they spoke among themselves, sounded like rain on
the tarp she used to pull over the pool at night in New
Hampshire. The sight of their vulnerable naked feet had
repelled her at first, like a snake might have. As she grew

used to it, though, she began to feel like washing them.

She waved to the guys in the guardhouse as she left the condominium complex—every single one of them seemed to have their teeth arranged wrongly—and stepped out to cross the street. Jaywalking wasn't illegal in Singapore, she had heard, if you were more than fifty meters from the lights. Everyone said meters. Actually, they said metres. Standing on the verge, she raised her hand to hail a cab. The air was thick and difficult to breathe. Eventually a light blue one pulled up, and the driver rolled down the passenger window.

"Where you go?" he demanded.

"Ramsgate?" she answered, and then screamed. Looking down, she saw that her feet, all the way to the ankles, were covered in a dense layer of tiny red ants. They had climbed her so lightly, and then, as if on command, had bitten her as one. "Ah! Ah! Ah!" she shouted, hopping around and batting them away. Her sunglasses fell to the ground, then her shoulder bag. Grabbing them both, she pulled open the cab door and sat on the seat with her feet outside, taking off her sandals and whacking them together to get rid of all the ants. When she finally pulled her legs inside and shut the door, the driver was smiling at her in the rearview mirror.

"I must have been standing on their nest," she told him, scratching her feet.

He shook his head and gestured with a gnarled hand.

"Why you not stand on driveway?"

Amy shrugged. She knew he was thinking *Crazy foreigner. Stupid, crazy foreigner.*

Amy felt a little lost when Elise was at school. In the morning she made the beds, washed the dishes, and hung out the laundry. It was unbelievable how long it took to dry. Summer in Nashua, you'd hang stuff out, it would flap a few times in the wind and you could bring it back in. Here it could take a few days, and even then it was still vaguely damp and smelled sour. She like the act of hanging it, though. Then she'd wonder what to do. Once a week she took delivery from a grocery provisioner who said he chose the freshest fruit and vegetables, and made recommendations from a list of foreign juices and yogurts. In New Hampshire, orange juice came from Florida. Period. In Singapore, it came from Australia, Malaysia, Malta. Malta? Sometimes the ingredients on the packages of the products she bought were translated into a dozen languages.

Singapore was so weird, but Dewey seemed to be thrilled by it. Actually, it wasn't so much Singapore as the heady responsibility of his new job with Seascape Oil. The company had offered him a place in New York, and Amy had had fun thinking about moving to Darien or New Canaan, but Dewey had voted for Singapore. "Please, Amy," he had said. "Can you do this for me?" He looked so excited. Of course she said yes, and worried about things quietly to herself, describing to Elise as often as she needed to hear it how close they'd be living to the ocean.

After she did her chores, Amy spent a lot of time at the broad, tinted living room windows, watching the gardeners beat the lush bushes back into their beds, scanning the tops of the trees for glimpses of the island's incredible, Popsicle-colored birds, watching the city disappear into storms that marched toward her like armies and obliterated everything.

What did other expatriate wives do? She was too shy to ask yet. Some of the other little girls in the complex had noticed Elise, and it was getting harder not to become involved with the people downstairs by the pool. Every few days Amy ended up in conversation with the mothers or the maids. She did so briefly, smiling, but all the while wondering as much about them as she did about the strange birds in the trees. Why did Australians pronounce the word "no" with more than one syllable? How could Chinese women bear to sit by and watch while the maid paddled with the baby in the pool? Didn't Indian women feel stifled by their long hair in the heat? She looked around nervously at Elise's potential playmates: pretty European girls whose Filipino maids bought them candy every day, little Japanese children clinging to their mothers, a white-blond girl attacking tadpoles in the pond by the parking lot while her mother wrote quietly in a journal under an

umbrella. To distract Elise from them, she took her to
the minimart to buy some local biscuits for them to try
upstairs. Usually they ended up wrinkling their noses and
throwing them away, opting instead for apples or Oreos.

It was always good to have Elise's hand in hers again.
They had the taxi drop them off at the condo gate. Hello
again to the guys in the guardhouse, who always seemed
to appreciate that. They walked back to their building
via the pool area, each slipping out of a sandal to test the
water. Maybe they'd swim after lunch.

"There's that boy," said Elise, pointing. They'd seen
him many times from their window, riding a bike that
was much too small for him, around and around and
around the winding paths between the buildings. He was
always alone. Even from twelve floors up Amy could see
how sharp his shoulder blades were as he leaned over his
handlebars.

This was the first time they had seen him while
downstairs, and since he didn't have his bicycle helmet
on, they could tell he was foreign. He was wearing a sun
suit—a bathing suit that covered the top of his body as well
as the bottom—and he was prowling. There was no other
word for it. Amy and Elise stopped walking and watched.
He was such an unusual-looking person, tiptoeing along
the edge of the pool like an elegant wetland bird. He
turned the corner at the far end of the pool and started

in their direction. When he saw them, his face seemed to open. The eyes that took them in were nearly as blue as the water in the pool, and were set impossibly wide apart. He approached.

"Do you know how a crocodile gets in the water?" he asked, sounding Australian, speaking more to Amy than to Elise. He pronounced each word very deliberately. Elise looked at her mother.

"I'm not sure," said Amy.

"Watch very carefully," the boy said slowly. He got down on all fours and moved, close to the hot ground, to the broad pool steps. He set his sights on an invisible quarry, then eased into the water with barely a ripple. He stayed under for a long time.

"Wow," whispered Elise.

"That was great," Amy told the boy when he emerged and stood in front of them. He pretended not to notice, shaking himself like a dog. He was pleased, though, she could tell. Pleased as punch.

"Watch me gallop like a horse," he said, and was off. His legs were like sticks, his knees knobby. His anklebones were strangely large, but still it was a wonder his feet didn't snap off his narrow shinbones as they slapped along the flagstones.

Amy started leading Elise to their building and he slowed to a trot and pulled up beside them. "How old are you, honey?" she asked him.

"Me? Oh, seven," he said.

"And what's your name?"

"Crispin."

"Well, it's nice to meet you Crispin. This is Elise." Elise looked over at the boy, peeking around her mother, but he didn't look back. Still on tiptoe, he was prowling again. Amy couldn't be sure, but she had the feeling he was looking around to see if anyone was watching him walk along with them. He looked as if he hoped so.

When they reached the sliding glass doors, he asked if he could come up with them.

"Where's your towel?" Amy asked him.

"My towel?" He hit himself on the head with his palm. "Oh. Um. Nowhere."

"How about your shoes?"

"I left them behind." He hit himself again.

"Well then, Crispin. Not this time. You're too wet. Anyway, we've got to have our lunch and a bit of a rest."

"You haven't had your lunch yet?!" he exclaimed in exaggerated shock.

"No, have you?" replied Amy, who was hungry, and getting tired of standing outside in the heat.

"Yeah. See? I burned my finger when I was cooking the hot dog."

"Nice to meet you, Crispin," said Amy, opening the glass doors with her key card and pressing the button for the elevator. Crispin stayed just outside the doors, his large

113

hands dangling in front of his chest like a begging dog.

"Where's he from?" asked Elise when they were preparing their tuna sandwiches.

"I can't tell," said Amy.

"Maybe Schenectady," said Elise. She loved this word.

"We'll have to ask him, I guess." Amy was uneasy. She had never known anyone who so immediately made her imagine heartbreak. She wondered what type of mother could send her seven-year-old child to the pool unaccompanied, could have him cook his own hot dog for lunch, could allow him to go without shoes in a country covered in red ants.

It was taking a long time for Amy to adjust. She found comfort a little too often in a milky instant coffee and some Fig Newtons—if she ate one she ate half the package—and was gaining weight. She had considered herself outgoing in Nashua. What had happened? She should pick up a hobby. In Nashua she had volunteered at the animal shelter, walking, feeding, and stroking the animals. Those had been her favorite days, other than Elise's birthdays and Christmas. Remembering this, she went to her bedside and opened the yellow pages to the SPCA. Looking at the phone number, she felt as if she had just swallowed a brick. Dialing the number, she heard the ocean in her ears.

The conversation she had with the woman who

answered was unintelligible, and she hung up with a lump in her throat. When Dewey came home that night she told him about the ordeal. "I couldn't understand the directions they gave me," she said.

"Maybe you should have asked them to say it in English," he suggested.

"We *were* speaking English!" she told him, and felt like crying again, but instead they laughed. Dewey could be so cute, though he'd seemed a little distracted lately. A couple of the people on his team at Seascape weren't pulling their weight.

"What do you think you'd like to do then, honey?" he asked her with a hug. He seemed to understand that she was unlikely to call the SPCA again.

"I don't know," she said. "Maybe swim?"

She went down to the pool twice the first week, three times the second, and four the third, working her way up to twelve lengths. One day, coming to the end of a length, she raised her head up from the water and found herself staring straight at Crispin's ankles. When she looked up he was gazing down at her with a twisted smile.

"What are you doing here, Crispin?"

"There's no school this week."

"Oh? Elise has school."

"I'm in a Singaporean school, though."

"Oh. So what are you going to do today?"

He shrugged. "Mummy sent me out for a bike ride, but I've already been riding for ages."

"Can't you go home?"

"Mummy's ill today."

Amy nodded, although she didn't really understand. "Well, I better finish my swim."

"What's your name?"

"Amy."

"Oh. Amy? Do you think, after your swim, I could come up for a little while?" He looked so worried. Seven-year-old children shouldn't have so many lines in their foreheads, she thought.

"Elise won't be there, you know."

He looked around. "I know."

"Well … can you read?"

His face brightened. "Yes. I'm a *great* reader."

"Let me finish my swim. Then you can come and read some of Elise's books, okay?"

"Okay! How much more are you doing?"

"Nine more."

"How long will that take?"

"Oh, I don't know, about fifteen minutes or so?"

Crispin looked at the big watch on his narrow wrist. He couldn't seem to tell time, though, because every few lengths he asked her again how many she had left.

Amy installed him in Elise's room and went to have her

shower. After dressing, she sat at her desk in the bedroom to write some e-mails home.

"Amy?" Crispin was standing in the doorway.

"Hello. Did you find some nice books?"

"Yes, but, um, do you think I could have something to eat?"

"Didn't you have any breakfast today?"

He shrugged. "Yeah."

"Come with me." She took him by the hand to the kitchen, sliced an apple, spread peanut butter on six Ritz crackers, and poured him a glass of milk. Once he was settled at the table, she left him to eat and went back to her correspondence.

"Amy?" He was at the door again.

"All done?" she called over her shoulder, not turning around.

"Well, I don't really like peanut butter all that much."

Suddenly she'd had enough. She swung around and said, "Crispin, honey, I invited you up here to read. I'm trying to get some things done." It didn't sound overly sharp to her, but he crumpled instantly and disappeared from the doorway. When she reached the living room he was already sitting on the floor putting his sandals on. His head hung down nearly between his knees.

"You don't have to leave," Amy told him. It was true. She couldn't bear the thought of his loneliness. But he left without another word.

A few afternoons later, Crispin was back, and then he came again, and again. When he buzzed from downstairs, Amy could see the top of his bicycle helmet in the video screen of the intercom. Elise was always delighted to see him. Lately, she had started playing with a little Danish girl a few floors above them, and though she clearly enjoyed their quiet make-believe, it was Crispin who excited her. When he came over, Elise hardly seemed to notice Amy at all as she stood in the middle of the living room, imploring the children to stop squealing so much. Amy felt the terror of the parents in the story of the Pied Piper as their children dropped everything and followed the piper without a backward glance. Crispin even dressed the part, often showing up wearing a hat of patchwork velvet.

His favorite game was pretending he was Elise's pet dinosaur. Elise would dote on him and follow the script he insisted upon. Amy tended to hover around them, interrupting the slightest unkindness or misunderstanding. When she finally admitted to herself that they were playing happily, she'd fold the laundry or make herself a cup of coffee.

Crispin didn't like it when she left them, though. More often than not, he'd figure out a way to follow Amy, inventing sillier and sillier antics to maintain her attention. She sensed that he kept the play noisy and fast so that they wouldn't interrupt him and ask him to leave. There were times during the games when Amy could hear Elise saying, "Crispin? Crispin? Why don't we—? Crispin!" She'd be on the verge of tears a few times each visit. Then Amy would tap him on the shoulder and say, "Please listen, Crispin. Elise is trying to talk to you."

"Crispin! It's time to go!" Amy called to him one day when he was being a baby Tyrannosaurus Rex. He had told her his mother wanted him home at five. He dropped his hands. There were lines on his forehead again. Amy crouched down by his side as he put on his sandals. "Is everything okay?" she asked.

"I've got to go," he said.

"Just let me tell you one thing first," she said. He didn't look at her, just sat still and waited. Amy pressed on. "We really like you. Even if you come over and just sit with us. Even if you don't say anything at all. You don't need to make jokes all the time. We really like you."

Crispin nodded. Amy stood up and so did he, giving her a quick sideways hug that forced his bony shoulder into her belly. He left again without saying goodbye.

E-mails from Nashua raved about the September weather. Amy remembered the first few days of school each year when everyone wore their new fall clothes even though it was still warm out. This year it was unusually cool, though, and the leaves were spectacular. That was the word everyone was using. Her best friend, Heather, asked in one message if the leaves turned in Singapore.

"They turn brown and fall off, and new ones grow in right away," Amy wrote back. "There are no bare branches in Singapore. And there are these amazing flowers all over, and they're always in bloom. There's one lady at the condo whose job is to sweep up the blooms that have fallen on the ground. Imagine that. She sweeps up all these pretty magenta flowers on the paths, and the next day she has to start all over again. I can't figure out if it's a good job or a bad job."

Without these messages from home, Amy wouldn't have remembered what month it was. It was always summer when she looked out the window. She worried a little that if she blinked, she'd miss Thanksgiving.

Crispin began showing up at the apartment every day, even when Amy told him not to come. There was always something he absolutely had to show Elise—either he had just received a new toy (these were all obviously old and worn), or he had drawn them a picture.

One Thursday, Amy faced the fact that she would have to call Crispin's mother. "What's your mommy's name, Crispin?" she asked him after he and Elise had begun a Lego tower in the living room.

"Meredith," he said, not looking up.

"Do you know your phone number?"

Now he looked up. "Four four oh seven nine oh seven."

"Okay. I'm just going to call her, make sure she knows where you are."

Crispin shrugged.

Amy went into her bedroom and perched on the edge of her bed and dialed. The voice that answered was like brass, with a heavy Australian accent.

"Hello?"

"Hello, this is Amy Mitchell, Elise's mother?"

"Oh, yes!" the woman said, sounding to Amy like "Ow, yiss!" "I've heard so much about you and your little girl."

"I see. Well—."

"Yes, Crispin talks my head off about you. He says he wishes you were his mother. Can you believe that?"

"Oh? Well, um, we really enjoy seeing him, but—."

"Yeah? Would you like me to send him over some time?"

Amy paused to catch her breath. "He's here every day, Meredith."

"He is? Well, you'd think he might of told me!"

"Yes, actually, I would."

"I'm sorry. I hope he's no trouble. We've had complaints, you know."

"Oh?"

"Yeah. He follows people around. They don't like that."

"Well, maybe if he weren't alone so much …"

Meredith didn't appear to get her meaning. "What?"

"It's just that he's on his own so much. Maybe there's not enough for him to do."

"Oh, no, he can go for bike rides, and he's got his Pokemon cards. No, he's just really annoying sometimes."

Amy felt winded again. She stood up and went to the bedroom window. Although it was firmly closed and locked, the broad view gave her the illusion of breathing space.

"He's fine," Amy told Meredith. "But he's here so often, I wonder if we can work out one day a week that is his day with Elise. Then maybe he can do other things for the rest of the time."

"Oh, okay. That's great. What day?"

"Say, Monday?"

"Monday it is, then. That's very kind. Come and have a coffee sometime, what'd you say your name was?"

"Amy."

"Amy. Well, what time is it? Four? God, I'm tired. Anyway, maybe you should send Crispin home now if he's bothering you."

"Oh, no, he's no trouble." There was a crash from the living room. Amy suspected that Crispin had destroyed the

Lego tower. "No trouble. I'll send him at five, okay?"

"That's great. Come for a coffee sometime."

Back in the living room, Elise was sitting with her knees pulled up to her chest, watching as Crispin used the Legos to build a fantasy world.

"Okay, Crispin," Amy said brightly, "your mommy and I have worked out that Monday is the best day for you to come over and play."

"How about Monday, Wednesday—"

"Just Monday, Crispin. You and Elise have other things to do on other days."

Crispin's hands went quiet and his huge eyes searched the room for something. "Amy?" he said slowly, "Do you think I could have something to eat?"

Although she knew he would be having his dinner in less than an hour, she prepared him a snack, and she and Elise watched as he ate half a mango and five slices of fresh banana bread.

Dewey had taken the morning off. He had his first business trip to Jakarta that afternoon. He accompanied Elise to school and helped Amy hang out the laundry. Then they sat and sipped the coffee she had made.

"I know it's not that far," Amy said, "but I feel like Jakarta might as well be Jupiter."

Dewey laughed. "I think it will be okay. Trying to keep Scott from saying anything stupid will keep my mind

123

off whether or not I'm using the right fork. If they even use forks there."

Now Amy laughed. "It's great to have you here."

"Great to be here. The weekdays just fly by, don't they?"

"They seem pretty long, actually. But still I feel like we only talk about five minutes a day."

Dewey put a hand on her cheek. "Yeah."

"And you don't get to read much to Elise in the evenings."

Dewey looked down and shrugged. "I'm here now, though," he said.

They picked Elise up from school together and swung their pretty little girl between them into the air with every few steps toward the building.

Crispin showed up as they were eating lunch, and Dewey bristled. "It *is* Monday," Amy told him quietly.

Dewey wiped his mouth with a paper napkin. "I'll go and pack, then," he said and went to the bedroom. Amy was torn between supervising the kids and helping Dewey choose his ties, but the decision was made for her when she heard her husband calling her name.

The children sidled into the bedroom not long afterward. Crispin started picking things up.

"What are these?" he asked from beside the bed.

"Those are ear plugs," Amy told him.

He put them in his nostrils.

Elise giggled, and Amy moved to pull them out, but Dewey said, "That's disgusting," before she got there. The boy replaced them on the bedside table in a flash. He waited to see if anything else would happen; then, when it didn't, he began to poke around again. Amy sat on the bed to fold a shirt Dewey was struggling with, and Dewey went back to his closet. Elise noticed a shopping bag by the wall.

"What's this, Mommy?" she asked, pulling something out.

Amy looked up. "That's my new swimsuit."

"Can I try it on?"

Amy laughed. "You don't need to. We know it won't fit you."

"Pleeeeeeeease?"

"Oh, okay."

Elise started to take off her shorts.

"Not here, Elise!" Amy said sharply. "Go in the bathroom, okay?"

When Amy got up to put the shirt in Dewey's suitcase, she realized that Crispin was moving toward the bathroom as well.

"Excuse us," he said as he flounced past Dewey. "We need a little privacy." He closed the door.

Dewey looked at the door and his eyes flashed. He took three strides to the bathroom, and threw the weight of both open hands against the door. "Open this door

NOW!" he bellowed. Amy had never heard him sound like this. A cowering Crispin crept out. Dewey took a step inside to see if Elise was okay. Crispin went and stood in the bedroom doorway, toes just over the threshold. His shoulders had caved; his chest was heaving. So was Dewey's.

Dewy put his hands on his hips and shook his head. He was handing things over to her, Amy knew, so she called to Elise and took Crispin by the hand, leading him to the living room. "How about doing a puzzle?" she said. He sat on the floor and stared at it. "Please, Crispin," she said, nearly whispering in her urgency. "Please just do a puzzle."

Amy was preparing tacos for dinner a week later. She had been amazed at how easy it was to find El Torito products in Singapore. Even the little cans of jalapenos. The lettuce and tomatoes probably came from Malaysia, and the ground beef and cheese came from Australia, but when she put it all together it would taste like an American meal.

Elise was watching CNN with Dewey. He always needed to catch the headlines at seven, and figured he could turn this into quality time with his daughter. He and Amy had agreed he would change the channel if the news included death by anything other than natural causes.

The phone rang. Amy picked up the portable receiver on the counter with the ends of her oniony fingers and secured it between her right cheek and shoulder.

"Amy? Hi. It's Meredith. Is Crispin there?"

"No, sorry. He wasn't here today. What's happened?"

"He ran away."

"You mean he packed up?"

"No, he just slipped out the door. Didn't even put his shoes on."

Amy looked out her kitchen window at the pale evening sky. "Well, if he comes here, I'll call you right away. How's that? Or do you want me to come down and help you look?"

"No, no. I'll send Honey down to find him."

"Who's Honey?"

"She's the maid."

"You have a maid?" It seemed odd that Honey never kept Crispin company either.

"Don't you?"

"No."

"I get so tired, you know."

"Are you sure you don't want me to look as well?"

"No. Thanks. I'll call again if I don't find him."

The phone rang again twenty minutes later, when they were all up to their wrists in taco sauce at the dinner table. Amy took the call in the kitchen, and could hear crying in the background.

"Do you think you could talk to him?" Meredith

asked.

Amy was alarmed. "Why?"

"His father's not home, and he won't listen to me."

"About what?"

"I've told him he's to go to bed without dinner, but he won't go."

"Well, what's he doing?"

"He's just sitting on the couch, watching TV, and he screams at me when I talk."

"Turn the TV off." This seemed so obvious.

"He turns it on again."

"Why is that allowed?" None of this was making sense. Amy knew without looking that Elise and Dewey were coming to the end of their dinners in the dining room. Everything was as it should be in their apartment. What had gone so wrong at Crispin's?

"I dunno. I can't stop him. Can you speak to him? Please?"

"Okay. If you think it will help."

Amy heard Meredith's voice say, "Speak to Amy," and imagined her holding the receiver out to her son.

"Hello?" came the small voice, followed by a few hiccupping gasps.

"What's happening, Crispin?"

More gasps.

"Why did you run away today without telling your mother where you were going?"

"I don't know." Amy could hear the shrug of his bony shoulders in his voice.

"Just wanted to get out, huh?"

A sniff.

"It's wrong, you know, honey? Your mother was very worried about you."

Nothing.

"You understand that, don't you? It was wrong?"

"Yes." His voice was miniscule.

"Do you know what the right thing is now?"

"No."

"You tell your mother how very sorry you are. You tell her you won't do it again, and that you really need your dinner."

"Okay."

"That's a good boy. That's a good, good boy. Now what's today? Friday? Next is the weekend, and then Monday, so we'll be seeing you soon, okay?"

"Okay."

Crispin put his mother back on, and as Meredith was saying her thanks and commenting on how abusive Crispin could be to her, Amy was wondering why she felt like a coward. Worse. She felt like a traitor.

Amy fell asleep to the sound of Dewey leafing through the *International Herald Tribune* next to her on the bed. She woke up when he took one of her hands in his, then the other, in an effort to unclench her fists.

"What is it, Ame?" He stroked the muscles bunched along her jaw.

Amy blinked, registering the way her bottom teeth were forcing themselves upwards. "How strange," she said.

"Any idea what it is?" Dewey asked, putting his paper on the floor.

"You know what, Dew?"

"What?"

"I think it's Crispin."

He nodded. "It's pathetic."

"It's more than pathetic to me. It's like, it's unbelievable. I couldn't have imagined that such a thing existed."

"Oh, yeah? Huh."

"I just wish it would go away."

"You don't have to see him, you know."

"I'd still worry about him, though. That wouldn't solve my problem."

Dewey exhaled through his nose and turned away from her. She knew he was going to say one more definitive thing and then turn out the light.

"Well," he said, "you're doing what you can."

The room went dark. Soon Dewey was asleep.


The Monday routine was working. Amy knew to have a big snack prepared for when Crispin showed up. If it was overcast she took the kids to the playground downstairs, where Crispin always seemed to need to show off a few of his tricks for her before settling down to play with Elise. In fact, Amy had the feeling that no matter what Crispin was doing he always had his antennae out to see if she was watching him. On terribly sunny days they'd stay indoors. Once she tried to get Crispin and Elise to draw together, but he specialized in designs of parent traps involving knives and penises. After that she let them devise their own games, and the three of them became more confident with each other.

One day Crispin came over with a present. It was a coloring rather than a drawing, a whole page full of birds. He had used colored pencils, and the picture showed a breathtaking amount of control, attention to detail, and imagination. The colors were so confidently applied that the page had curled. Amy could tell that he was pleased by the level of her astonishment, as if he had revealed to her his secret and now knew that he had done the right thing.

"Would you like to stay and play?" she asked him. It wasn't a Monday. She looked at Elise, who shrugged, but nodded.

"Would I?!" he said excitedly, exaggeratedly, and galloped around the couch.

"I'll just call your mom, then," Amy said.

On the phone, she told Meredith how lovely she thought the coloring was. "I don't think there are many seven-year-olds who could accomplish a picture like this," she said honestly.

"Yes," said Meredith. "I'm very proud of him. But *I* did the parrot."

"What day is it, Mommy?" Elise asked as they walked home from the taxi after school.

"It's Monday, honey."

"Oh," Elise said with the drawn out, rising tone children use to express disappointment.

"What?"

"I don't want to play with Crispin today."

"No?"

"I want to play with Marid."

"Marid has ballet today."

"Just you, then."

"Why, sweetheart?"

"I just don't want to play with Crispin."

"Kinda need a break?"

Elise nodded.

Amy was a little worried as they left the pool behind. Sometimes Crispin was waiting for them when they reached the glass doors of the building. She knew not to force Elise to play with him, but couldn't think of what to tell him if he was there, eyes bright and shining in anticipation.

He wasn't there. As they went up in the elevator, Amy asked Elise, "Would you like me to call Meredith and see if we can take a few weeks off?"

Elise nodded again, not smiling, but clearly grateful.

Amy got on the phone. "Hello, Meredith? Hi. It's about Crispin."

"Yeah, I should of called you. He won't be coming over today."

"No?"

"No, he's done something so naughty, I'm keeping him home."

Amy had heard this before, when Crispin lost his scooter. She knew Meredith wanted to tell her what had happened, and that Crispin was probably within earshot. She wished she could hang up immediately.

"We've been having a problem with him at school. A parent complained, see. He's been taking another boy's penis out of his pants and fondling him."

"Oh, dear God."

"I know. His father gave him a right thrashing."

"Meredith!"

"And I said to him, 'Crispin, how could you do something so *dirty*?'"

"Stop, Meredith! Stop! You're shaming him! Don't you see? He doesn't know what he's doing. How's he supposed to tell you?"

Amy felt the atmosphere change on the other end of the line as Meredith backtracked.

"Well, of course, I took him aside and said, 'Crispin, darling, what's wrong? Where's my lovely boy? Where's my good Crispin?"

"For God's sake, Meredith! You can't have it both ways!"

"I know. I know. We'll see what happens. I've got an appointment with the school psychologist next Thursday."

"Meredith," Amy said firmly, her eyes feeling red hot. "Somewhere along the line Crispin has been damaged, and I think you've got to figure out how to heal him."

"I think I know when it happened," said the woman without missing a beat. Amy felt momentarily as if fresh air had entered the tunnel she was stuck in. "I think it was when he was a baby, and we were staying with his father's parents."

"What?"

"Yeah. I left him with them for a bit, to do some shopping or something, and when I came back they had tied him down with Velcro. Said he was moving about too much. 'Don't you *ever* tie my child up again,' I told them, but I'm sure he suffered."

"Send him over tomorrow," Amy said, "if you feel it's okay."

Amy and Elise were eating dinner when the doorbell rang that night. When Amy opened the door, Crispin slipped in like a shadow and stood panting, barefoot, by the shoe tree. Without a word, Amy took him to the table and served him the pork chop meant for Dewey. She waited, feeling as if her ear holes were widening with the effort, for the phone to ring. But it didn't. It never did.

This time Crispin didn't talk, and Amy didn't try to draw him out. After dinner she put him in front of the television while she bathed Elise, who was solemn, and seemed to know it would be unwise to complain.

With Elise in bed, Amy ran a bath for the boy. She turned off the television and took his hand to lead him to the bathroom. "Do you know how to bathe yourself?" she asked him as he stood on the unfamiliar bathmat.

He nodded.

"Okay," she said. "Here's your towel."

"But my mother usually helps me."

The entreaty was painfully clear. Amy didn't want Crispin to feel any hesitation from her. "All right, then," she said, and pulled his t-shirt up over his head, not letting herself stare at the hungry maw of his ribcage. He flinched when she took hold of his shorts, and she had to tug to get them down between his locked knees. He wasn't wearing any underpants, and immediately covered his little penis with his hands before turning to step into the water.

Amy didn't gasp when she saw the bruises on his thighs and shy buttocks, since her conversation with Meredith had prepared her for them.

Crispin sat folded up on himself while Amy washed

his back, bumping up and down along his vertebrae. He winced when she pushed him gently backwards so he would lean against the rim of the tub while she washed one long, grimy foot after the other. She took time over his knobby toes, scraping the dirt from the edges of his toenails with a fingernail. She rubbed his knees until they were red, then turned on the tap to get clean water for his face. When she shampooed his hair, she felt he wanted to relax but didn't dare.

"There," she said, and pulled the plug. She held up the towel so he could hide behind it as he climbed out. When she wrapped it around him he leaned against her, and they both exhaled. "It'll be okay," she said.

When the apartment door opened and closed, they stiffened. "Stay right here," she said.

Dewey was taking off his shoes by the door. Amy realized she had tears on her face as she crossed the living room to meet him.

"Whoa. What's wrong?" She took him by the shoulders, much more to steady herself than to prepare him for what she had to say.

"It's Crispin."

"Oh, for Christ's sake."

She took him by the hand and pulled his reluctant weight through the living room, through the bedroom, and into the bathroom.

It was empty. Amy turned and stepped back into

the bedroom.

Crispin stood silently by the bed with the ear plugs in his ears. He had let the towel fall to the floor around his feet, it had been so important to him to cover his eyes as well.

# Strays

I live on my own in Singapore with three big dogs. Two was enough, but then we left Biggo and Maya together by mistake for an afternoon. That was before Ward moved out. For a while we had seven dogs, and I wiped and scraped and mopped the floor at least twice every day. Each time I handled the puppies' soft bodies, marveling at how loosely attached their tiny bones felt under their skin, I thought of India.

I remembered the cold rain at Delhi's Red Fort, and some nearby slaughtered goats. And crying tears of astonishment at the sight of the Taj Mahal at dawn: the mist like the marble monument's own breath. And being pushed out of the way by an irritated cow on a narrow street in Jaipur; and a night in the Thar Desert when I watched a solitary crab making tracks across sand turned blue by the moon. But the moment I always remembered first took place in Jaisalmer.

From a distance, Jaisalmer looks like a sand castle. You must enter the town to accept that it is really made of stone and that its turrets will not crumble when you step inside them. From our guesthouse there, Ward and I viewed the army's camel corps going through its drills. We walked the cobbled streets looking at silver being sold out of large holes in the fortified walls and dodging sewage pouring out of smaller ones. We stepped over animals in every alley, and once had to negotiate with an intense young man to get him to coax his cow out of our way. The old rubber flip-flop on a rope around her neck was intended, he told us, to protect her from the envious evil eye of his neighbors.

India was teeming with bewildered beasts: mangy bitches with engorged nipples practically dragging in the dust, monkeys carrying on with their thieving ways, even with mutilated limbs. And one day, in Jaisalmer, there was a puppy in a sunny courtyard, straining in utter incomprehension at the task of passing his own shining bowels.

"Oh, my God," I said to Ward. I couldn't look. Never breaking his stride, Ward studied the wretched creature. On his face he wore half a smile. I both envied and deplored his ability to watch without averting his eyes.

"It's going to die, right?" I said.

"Absolutely," he replied.

Ward finally looked away. Lunch was the next thing on the agenda, but I couldn't think about it. I turned and ran back to the puppy. My eyes wouldn't allow for details.

I refused to see more than the little animal's outline against the sandy paving stones. Even now I can't say if it had the time to look at me in surprise as I bore down on it. But I will never forget the pressure of its perfect jaw against my left palm and of its miniature shoulder blade against my right, or the way its skin slipped as I broke its neck.

Biggo is really Ward's dog. We found him in the classifieds. Two middle-aged Chinese sisters came to the door at the address on the ad and invited us through their cute little house to the back garden, where a husky was tied to the fence. At the sight of us Biggo leaped and barked, straining his heavy rope.

"Shut up!" the slightly larger sister barked back, advancing. "Quiet!" She did her best to calm him down, throwing a few looks over her shoulder at us that clearly said, "You see how difficult he is for me?"

"If you can handle him, you can have him," said the other sister hopefully.

It appeared to me that the dog gave Ward a similar hopeful look as Ward approached him with his long stride. My husband took him by the collar and stared him down, keeping him planted on the ground when he tried to jump. Then he did some rough scratching around the dog's head and neck. Biggo barked but never once looked to his owners for any form of reassurance as Ward took possession of him.

ALISON JEAN LESTER

I actually grew up afraid of dogs, although no one in my family can trace the fear to an incident. For some reason, I believed that dogs could overwhelm me. I was comforted by the disdain of cats, but couldn't read a dog's eyes. When a golden retriever pinned me to a wall with his front paws, what did he want? There were too many possible answers.

"You just slap him," Ward always told me, but I couldn't imagine ever doing that.

All the same, Maya, the red setter, is my dog. I saw her several times in the park, loping diffidently around, catching a whiff of Biggo but keeping her distance, before I went back there alone and brought her home. She was emaciated and nervous, with flaky skin and some nasty sores on her neck where a rope or chain must have been. She had worms in her heart and crust on her eyes. I cleaned her up, little by little, and little by little she became mine.

I am not particularly social these days, but I do find myself in the frequent company of Ruby, the Chinese lady who lives in a cement house identical to mine, on the other side of my eastern wall. I often feel about Ruby the same way you feel when you get hit by bird shit: *If only I had left the house half a second earlier it would have missed me.* She has yellow fingernails, dirty gray hair in a tidy bun behind her neck, and a single fascinating tooth. No matter what she comes over to tell me, I hear it coming directly from the tooth. It's big and tall and turning brown, and unlike Ruby it stands up straight.

"Mrs. Ward!" she calls out from the front step. She pretends not to know that Ward and I are separated, and sometimes when he has left after a more or less civil cup of tea and some wrestling with Biggo, she comes over bearing a gift—peanuts she's been given but can't eat, a single can of a lurid soft drink—and delivers her take on things.

"Mr. Ward is looking very anxious these days," she'll say.

She's right. When he comes over he greets the dogs with the only effusion I've ever seen from him, but when he goes out back with Biggo, the play winds down quickly, as if it had been simply for my benefit. Sometimes I see him sitting on the bricks of the barbeque he built, head and hands hanging. Biggo sits at attention, waiting to catch his eye again.

"How do you know he's anxious?" I ask Ruby.

"He nearly hit his head getting into the taxi."

Ruby watches Ward leave. I don't.

"You work so hard, Mrs. Ward, so hard," she says, whacking me on the back in her way of showing affection without showing affection. It's true, I do. My two-person editing company, The English Merchant, has recently become popular. My income is stable, my rent is low. The dogs need me, and apparently so does Ruby. I never seriously imagine packing up and heading back to DC.

143

I'm trying to fill my watering can from the trickle of water my kitchen can cough up. This reasonable, run-of-the-mill Singaporean house was charming to me when we moved in, but the charm wore off when I realized what a lazy house it is. Ruby keeps whacking me as we watch the water together. Then she stops and sniffs loudly. "They've attacked my fence again," she says as we pad barefoot across the cool tiles of the living room, put on outdoor slippers, and step onto the short driveway.

"Oh?" I say noncommittally, but before I can bend to water the bougainvillaea bushes around my doorway she's pulling me by the sleeve over to the fence between her driveway and mine, pointing.

"It just looks rusty to me, Ruby," I tell her, as I do every time, but she's shaking her head.

"They throw acid on it to burn a hole."

Ruby's house is the only one of the row that my landlord, Mr. Eng, hasn't been able to buy, and she believes he is just waiting for her to die so he can tear them all down.

He is.

"They want to frighten me. Maybe they want to kill my cats, Mrs. Ward."

"I'm keeping an eye on you, Ruby, don't you worry."

She whacks me on the back again. "You come," she says. Other than tending the plants and running the dogs, I have no plans, so I calm myself, put down my watering can, and follow her out of my gate and through hers. Cats lurk in the shade of dusty weeds along the inside of the fence. Her one and only dog, Chapati, appears from nowhere, tapping over to Ruby on long brown toenails that look stronger than his leg bones. She speaks to him, but keeps on walking, dribbling him like a soccer ball toward her door.

Singaporean houses are built to be dark and cool. In Ruby's and mine, the sun never manages a direct hit on either of our first floors because of the overhangs in the front and the heavy frosting on the jalousies in the back. The concrete walls between the rooms end six inches before the ceiling for airflow and a little light. It's perpetual twilight in my house, but in Ruby's it's midnight. While my living room is vaguely like a warehouse, hers gives the impression of an air-raid shelter long after peace has been reestablished, and she has the trademark yellow piles of newspaper of people who are willingly overrun with animals. I want to leave her front door open to let in more sun, but she steps back around me to close it before proceeding. I have to stay right behind her to navigate my way to the stairs, stepping on Chapati in the process. He yelps, but Ruby doesn't even turn around. Her trajectory is not to be interrupted. She is taking me to her bedroom.

She goes straight to her wardrobe and opens it. Something seems amiss when a swarm of ghostly moths doesn't come puffing out. Everything stays too still. The sagging bed looks despondent, and the two cats sprawling on it appear dead. Only Ruby and her hunched back seem alive, somehow, and mobile. She's pawing through the clothes hanging before her. "You need dresses, Mrs. Ward," she informs me, pulling out a few with a powdery, slithering sound. "This one's lovely." She holds up a pale green one with a draped bosom, a rusty stain like a tire track at the waist and a rip running diagonally across the hip, revealing the ivory lining as if it were bone. "You wear this one to dinner with a shawl."

On the wall near the wardrobe is a black and white studio portrait of a young Chinese woman with ornaments in her tightly coiffed hair. She frowns purposefully for the camera with dark painted lips, covering up for appearing hopeful. I step in for a closer look. It is clear her embroidered cheongsam is well tailored, and her bracelet is certainly jade. I find it a challenge to associate the woman in the photo with my nut-brown neighbor, so I ask, "Is this you, Ruby?"

She pretends she hasn't noticed me peering at the photo. "Is what?"

"This photo."

She glances at it briefly with a little wince and returns to rooting in the wardrobe. "Maybe," she says. "Maybe not. Don't remember. Don't know who put that there."

Ruby eventually presses seven old dresses on me. I have to take them. I walk back downstairs with an armload of Ruby's life.

A few days later, I walk along the road from the bus stop thinking about how great it will be to get out of my pumps and suit, how calming (once the dogs have settled down again) to put on some music and water the plants. I let Maya and Calamansi, the puppy we kept, out onto the cement of the small front yard, and go upstairs to change. Biggo is barking in the back yard. When I come back down, Ruby is sitting with Maya and Calamansi on the front step. When they're seated side by side, Maya is taller than Ruby. Ruby is pulling apart what looks like a sandwich and feeding it to the dogs, who take the pieces daintily from her. Anyone else, including me sometimes, they would pin to the ground.

When I approach, the dogs get up and nuzzle me, then whack me with their wagging tails as they turn around and head back to Ruby.

"Your dogs love kaya, Mrs. Ward," she tells me. "Now I have only one piece for you."

"Oh, that's okay," I tell her. "I have to go out to dinner anyway. Thanks, though." She gets up and follows me inside with the dogs, as if she is one of them. Now she's pulling the kaya bread apart for me.

"You work so hard, Mrs. Ward. Need to eat." She's trying to push some bread into my mouth. I usually like the thick, greeny, egg and coconut spread, but I'm not at

147

all in the mood.

"I've got to water the plants first. And walk the dogs."

"Eat," Ruby insists.

I try to concentrate on the relief of the cool stone beneath my naked feet as I accept the snack the tiny, smelly woman is feeding me. Finally gratified, she goes out back and talks to Biggo while I water out front; then she returns home.

Later, I stand in front of my closet wondering what to wear for the evening. I've hung my tangerine linen suit next to Ruby's old dresses, which still look dusty although I've beaten and aired them. I've decided to take them to the Salvation Army, but now I pull out the black knitted one with the V of black lace between collarbone and cleavage. It would have been an appropriate midcalf length on Ruby, but now it appropriately skims my knee. I have to shorten my bra straps to hoist my breasts into the dress's darts, and I have to spray an unusual amount of perfume not to smell musty. I put on a black half-slip so that no one will see my skin peeking out through the two moth holes, then leave the house feeling no more or less comfortable than usual, hoping Ruby is watching in the gathering gloom.

I want to ask her why she is alone. I want to ask her if she was ruined by an Indian, like me.

His name was Ramana, and he engaged The English

Merchant to rectify some text for a documentary about Singapore's budding theater for the deaf. He initially contacted us by email, so I was unaware that he was deaf himself until he came to the office and began signing to me.

There's something so sexy about sign language; it insists that people communicate by touching themselves. Watching Ramana sign so boldly at me made me feel shy and stupid. I put up my hands in a smiling gesture that meant, "I'm sorry. I'm an idiot." He scribbled on his left palm with his right index finger, eyebrows raised. I gestured him to the chair by my desk and pulled out a pad and pen, passing them over. My heart skipped several beats as he took my pen in his long black fingers and I waited to see what he might write.

He passed the pad back to me. "You have VCR?" it said on it. I was disappointed. I think I had been expecting a sonnet.

I nodded and stood up, putting out a hand to keep him in his seat. Our office is so small that the things we need on a less-than-regular basis, like the television, the coffee maker, the calculator, and sanitary napkins, must be pulled out of somewhere. We hadn't done text for a video in a while. Usually when we did, my partner, Hwee Koon, was in charge of making sure our English faithfully matched the Chinese dialogue. This time the dialogue would be remote to us both. I was excited at the prospect that Ramana would have to stay involved to respond to my constant but unspoken question: "Is this what you meant?"

I heaved our little Aiwa set out of a cupboard and put it on the edge of my desk. Ramana's eyes lit up. He seemed to be enjoying himself, which gave me confidence as I plugged in the cord.

We watched. I wasn't sure how to go about things. He had handed me the intended text on paper. Perhaps he expected me to be referring to it during the program, as he kept shooting me looks. I smiled back but tried to maintain an expression on my face that said, "This is exactly how we do things."

In the sign language alphabet "o" and "k" look like themselves, and Ramana also mouthed the letters for me, producing a noise reminiscent of the music we made as children with a comb and a piece of waxed paper. I understood his question, and the rush of pleasure made my face tingle. I answered with exaggerated nodding, although I hadn't understood a moment of his film.

For the remainder of that day, I thought about how Ramana squeaked and buzzed at me like something from another planet. I felt as if I could have touched him and divined his meaning. All I needed was to touch him.

There was a moment before every time Ward touched me, a cushion of time and air in between his intimating the impulse and carrying it out, which was infused with distrust and indecision. He'd lift one arm as a question, and I'd hug him in answer. Or I'd feel him walk up behind me in the park, watching the dogs, and I'd be aware of his hands hovering above my shoulders for a while before he chose for them to fall. We both held our breath.

The way he approached love sideways and flicked his eyes around at the walls and windows made me feel as if I had tempted a deer indoors. A deer that had never imagined how nice it could be to be fed and stroked, that had a dim recollection of nuzzling its mother for milk but was constantly assessing escape routes.

It was convenient to be able to explain to Ward that I had bought sign-language flash cards because of a new contract rather than because I wanted more than emails from a compelling acquaintance. I learned the alphabet quite fast, as well as "am," "have," "want," and "know." The rest of the flash cards were ridiculous. While almost every other language would offer words with which to construct sentences like "This is my wife" and "Do you like coffee?" these flash cards offered words to put together like "People make lots of orange pigs" and "Maybe small boats are blue." I annoyed Ward by gesticulating this type of nonsense in bed, making myself chuckle while he was trying to read and sleep. He had been amused the first night but naturally couldn't fathom why the effort was so consistently entertaining to me.

When I was halfway through the work, four or five days after our first meeting, I asked Ramana to come and see me. My experience has been that clients who set their own schedules don't want the work finished immediately. Grunts who are sent to me in order to please someone else call twice a day, but people on the top of projects, like Ramana, feel better when time is taken. In fact, I could have corrected the text in about forty minutes. Instead, I cultivated my vocabulary ("Wash dishes!" "I can climb tree.") and went again and again through the video, looking for signs I knew. It was a puzzle. I peeled my eyes for signs I could identify, then sought them in the text. I wanted the spoken English to have the same feel as the signs. I put them together, trying to make them click into place. It was a labor of love.

Ramana's appointment was for the end of the day. I wanted Hwee Koon to leave, but I needed her there to show myself how professionally I was behaving. Before Ramana arrived I handed her a two-page job that I had corrected and needed her to approve for local consumption. So she sat at her desk, every bit of her intelligence nicely organized, every sleek hair in place, while I sat at mine, sweating a little and internally unkempt.

He walked in with his combination of slouching and loping that made him look constantly on the verge of dancing, sat down, and smiled. His lower lip curled out and down, revealing a slim shimmer of the wet interior of his mouth.

We did the work. He smiled approvingly, and looked at me as if I were really cute when I mimicked the signs I had memorized to impress him. I *felt* really cute. I felt shy, less of an idiot, and also daring.

No doubt days passed between this and our next meeting, and then more days before we met again, but in my mind now these meetings occur without breaks. Like fireworks. You know there are always spaces between fireworks, when you are aware they've been launched but hold your breath for their explosion. But once the fireworks bloom and tattoo themselves on your mind, the pauses fall away. In my mind Ramana sits and smiles in my office, and immediately thereafter we are beaming at each other across a table crowded with biryani and curries at his parents' apartment. His father is infirm, shuffling out of his room wrapped in white, sitting briefly out of politeness, shuffling back to bed. His mother is busy in the kitchen, busy bringing us food, busy signing for us to eat—she can hear, but when she speaks she speaks Tamil. Ramana winks at me, offering a handful of rice from his own plate.

Ward is travelling on business. I imagine him leaning into a cold Korean wind, chopping through complicated negotiations with his sharp brain. I try to think of my relationship with Ramana as business-based. This is a business dinner. This might lead to more work.

"You want to make more V-I-D-E-O-S?" I sign, doing business.

He bobs his right fist, "Yes," then smiles as he continues eating. Then he wipes his hands to sign, "You be S-T-A-R."

"Me?"

"Wear a B-I-K-I-N-I."

"I will if you will."

We are signing freely. His father is in bed, and his mother can't see us as she stirs away in the kitchen. Were Ramana not deaf, we might have to whisper. I can hear our words in my head, but no one else in the apartment can hear anything we are saying.

Immediately next in my memory I am in my kitchen making tea we won't drink. I hear Ramana breathing into my hair. I hear his bracelet ping against my belt buckle as he encircles me with his arms. I hear his breathing change, although he can't hear it. When I turn on the computer to print the final copy of my work for him, he sits me on his lap. When he licks my ear, I alone hear myself moan, and my moans take on a different meaning. All the noises I normally make as encouragement become useless. I utter only what forces its way out, squirming on his thighs to communicate instead.

"What color?" he signs, pointing to my nipple through my shirt. I give him a peek and he kisses me there.

"What color?" I mirror, and he unbuttons his shirt enough to pull one side away and reveal a slice of skin and its dark velvet aureole. He lifts one hand to my face. "B-I-T-E."

He gasps with a sound like the striking of a match. I tie my dying marriage to a stake and light the fire that will burn it to the ground.


No one said a word after Ward discovered us. Ramana stood up from our position on the living room floor and went to the small bathroom by the stairs, half his body disappearing into the dark as he leaned in for a wad of toilet paper, which he gave to me. I was powerless to use it, and simply sat up, panty-less but otherwise discreet, and watched him slip back into his clothes. I heard his zipper, his belt buckle, the whisper of his T-shirt, the padding of his feet as he loped past Ward's crackling atmosphere. When he reached the open door he turned to look at me, and although his eyes showed confusion he gave me the Indian head wag. Maybe he meant, "It'll be fine" or, "Don't worry about me" or something, but three weeks in India and three more with Ramana couldn't accustom me to the gesture. To me it always looked like, "Who really gives a shit?"

I was still sitting on the floor when Ward left. It was nice and cool there. I was very, very tired.

I haven't seen Ramana since then. In the evenings I hear pots rattling in the kitchens of the other houses in this row. I hear the growls of my dogs after their dinner as they vie for their favorite positions on the rug in front of the couch. I hear the mobile phones of people walking home, and gates clanking and being locked.

In the mornings, just before six, I hear the lunatic call of koels—large, keening birds hiding in the tops of trees across the road. A little while later, Ruby begins to cough in the pitch dark of her bedroom. She's coughing for longer and longer spells. The muscles of my own abdomen and the lining of my throat ache in sympathy. Just a few days ago she came over to tell me about a new leak in her bathroom ceiling. Now, it seems, they are trying to spy on her while she is on the toilet. I couldn't register what she was saying right away because I was fixated on her tooth. It looked as if it were loose, and it required all my attention to ascertain whether or not this was so. It was. The tooth no longer looked like something that had grown up out of her gum but rather like something that had been inexpertly pushed in, like a fence post in mud.

When I finally understood what she was saying I told her my bathroom ceiling leaked as well at times.

"No!" she exclaimed.

"Sure," I told her, wondering if I should buy her a blender for her food, until I remembered she didn't have electricity in her house.

Suddenly her face cracked into sections determined by wrinkles. Her shoulders slumped and she began tapping one of her little feet at a hectic pace. I realized she was crying.

"Come, Ruby. Sit down," I said, guiding her to the couch. I patted her for a while. She was a lot bonier than her baggy T-shirts made her look. "No one's trying to get me, Ruby."

"Maybe by mistake."

"What?"

"Maybe they pick a hole through the wrong roof sometimes."

I laughed. "Let me call you a plumber, get your pipes looked at. Okay? He can put some fresh plaster on the ceiling, too."

Ruby put her hands over her face, and I thought she was going to cry some more, but she wiped away her tears and seemed to reconstruct her skin in one efficient motion. She pushed herself up off the couch and rocked on her bandy legs toward the door. *When the tooth falls out*, I thought, making myself smile, *she'll blame the plumber for poisoning her water.*

But as I heard her fasten the chains on her gate, I realized she would get worse. It wouldn't be funny when the tooth fell out, it would be heartbreaking. What was more, it would be impossible to get her to see a doctor for her cough. Neither she nor her house was going to get any

157

cleaner, and she'd be furious if I put a sign on her fence asking people to stop leaving unwanted kittens in boxes outside it.

The idea that I might have ordinary neighbors on both sides one day was nearly unbearable. I tried to think of Ruby living forever, of nothing changing, of cool floors and bougainvillea around the door and Ruby and my dogs teasing each other. Just as I thought I had accomplished this, I had an image of myself at Ruby's bedside, helping her die.

# Singapore Sting

My neighbor Jody and I were pretty sure our sting operation to entrap the plumber would be a success. The only problem was, we didn't realize we were dealing with the Chinese mafia.

Why should we? First of all, everyone knows Singapore is the safest place on earth. Second of all, the guy who came over to look at my sink was the sorriest Singaporean I'd ever met. Sorrier even than the old guy in droopy shorts with his life in tattoos all over his body like stickers on a suitcase, the one who hangs out at the food court over by the old fire station. That guy only wears shorts. Must have been in the merchant marine. He drinks and then sleeps with his head on the table. I'd still call him attractive. He's art. No shoes, but more than a shred of dignity.

Not this guy. This guy had shoes, but he was so skinny that the waist of his trousers slipped down to his hips, and he walked on his hems. Only a couple of teeth, so his lips kept disappearing. Probably fifty years old, which would mean he was born after the Japanese occupation, so he probably hadn't seen his father or grandfather dragged to prison camp or his mother raped or otherwise humiliated. Which meant I couldn't blame his nervous eye movements on the war.

I had asked this guy's boss, Mr. Li, to send him to my place on the pretense of needing advice on my sink, but actually because he had made a mess of Jody's sink, had overcharged her, and hadn't given her a receipt, so she had no proof. She also believed that he had deliberately sabotaged her toilet while she wasn't looking so that he had to come back. Now she wanted revenge.

In between his visit to her and to me, Jody, who has the character of a Jack Russell terrier, called Mr. Li many times to ask for a receipt and he always put her off. She went to the office address listed in the phone book, and it didn't exist. She called the Plumbers' Association, she called the Consumers' Association, she called the police, she called the tax authorities, and they all said they would be delighted if she could help nab him, because they couldn't. No proof. Every time she was told she couldn't be helped, she said, "Well, now I know how to make money in this country. Don't register a company, offer a service, take cash, and give no receipts."

We figured that this plumbing operation preyed on ignorant housewives who didn't think to ask for the laborer's identification card because this is the safest place on earth and didn't mind not having a receipt until the toilet fell out of the wall. We got it into our heads to expose the operation.

Once I had the appointment and the guy was due to arrive, Jody and her husband Imran left their baby with their maid and came over. I dripped water on the floor of the cabinet under my kitchen sink to simulate a leak. We set up my video camera on the far side of the living room, and Jody and Imran retreated to the guest room to spy through the crack between the door and the door jamb and listen. I buzzed the plumber in and let the camera roll.

I was scared. Jody's righteous indignation had permeated far enough into me to get me to accept the challenge, but not enough to eliminate my fear of angering men I didn't know. I'd had a stalker in Washington, working right there at the Commerce Department with me, taking the taxpayers' money from nine to five then leaving sick notes under my windshield wipers after hours. When one of the businesses I'd advised on investment in Singapore offered me a position, I said yes before they finished the sentence.

So I was short of breath and clammy-handed as I waited alone in the living room for the doorbell to ring. But the walking cadaver who came to my door simply didn't look like a con man. I showed him the recently moistened stain under my sink. It took him only a few seconds to tell me that my whole faucet unit needed replacing and he could do the job for 180 Singapore dollars. I showed him back into the living room, where I repeated his offer for the benefit of the camera, thanked him for his advice, and told him I'd like to get a second opinion.

His face collapsed. His big hands twitched. I had so much adrenalin running through my body from the lying that I could hardly breathe. This was where Jody was supposed to come out and ask him for a receipt and some identification, but she didn't because he wasn't fixing to go yet. He was looking around like a cow in a slaughterhouse.

"Okay, I can do one-fifty," he said.

"That's okay, thanks," I said. "I want to check with another contractor."

"One-thirty."

"Why would I pay when I'm not sure I want the work done?"

"Just one-thirty. Very cheap!" He was getting desperate.

"I'm not sure, so I'm not paying, okay? Thanks."

Now Jody came out.

"Hi," she said, "remember me?"

I honestly don't think he did. I suspect the reason he looked like he could have crapped is that he'd never in his wretched life been confronted by not one but two foreign women at once. I could practically feel the saliva drain out of his mouth.

"You came to my house and worked on my sink and toilet, but you forgot to give me a receipt. And I forgot to get any identification. So I've typed up a receipt for you. Can you just sign it for me, and show me some ID?"

"My ID is with the guard."

Damn. We'd forgotten that workmen had to leave their ID cards at the guardhouse when they came to the condo.

"Never mind. You can just sign, and write your ID number under your signature. Are you sure you don't remember me?"

He shook his head. Then he pulled out his phone and called Mr. Li. They spoke to each other in Hokkien, a Chinese dialect that sounds even more like music played backward than Swedish does. Then suddenly he handed me the phone.

"He'll do the job for one twenty-five," said the powerful voice.

"But I want another opinion."

"Just let him do it. It's a good price."

"But I'm not sure it's the right advice."

"Let him do it."

"No, thanks."

"One-twenty."

"You can't talk me into it."

He breathed out through his teeth.

"Just give him thirty dollars then."

"Why?"

"For the house call."

"You're kidding."

"No. Pay him for coming over."

"I don't have much cash. I can give him a check."

"No! He can't take a check. It's got to be cash."

"Why?"

"It's the weekend. The bank's closed. These type of guys, they need cash."

Jody mouthed to me that she had some, then pointed to her receipt.

"So is your guy going to sign this receipt?" I asked Mr. Li, feeling like a kidnapper, even though I was the one who'd just agreed to pay ransom.

"What for she needs a receipt?"

"You have a problem with that?"

Again the teeth breath.

Our resident cadaver was doing an excellent impression of a schoolboy who hasn't done his homework and is praying to Buddha that the teacher won't notice him.

"Okay, okay. He can sign. But give him the cash."

"Okay."

"Let me talk to him."

I handed the phone back and heard our man getting his orders. He hung up, signed the receipt, and added his ID number underneath. We paid him and watched him take his scrawny self back out of the apartment.

Imran came out of the guest room. While I turned off the camera, Jody compared the ID number to the one written on the copy of the cashed check she had received from her bank. It was the same guy, and the same number.

"Clever of Mr. Li not to sign it himself, isn't it?" I said.

"Yeah. I don't know how we're going to get him. He brings housewives to tears with his threats, you know."

"I can imagine. He might have cowed me, if it had been in person instead of on the phone."

"Shit. I guess this is a start, though."

I rewound the tape.

"Thing is," I said, "that guy who came here, he's no plumber. He doesn't know anything. So if he doesn't work for this bad guy, who'll employ him? Maybe he has a family."

"He's made some sorry choices," said Imran, who always says helpful things when he finally chooses to speak.

Jody used to work in PR before the baby, so she talked to someone in the press who agreed to write a story about scams like Mr. Li's. The journalist came to interview her, and Jody described the way she'd been deceived, referring to Mr. Li's advertisement in the paper so people would avoid it. To protect Jody's identity, the journalist gave her a fake name and took her photo from behind.

Jody also gave the name and ID number of the plumber we'd rumbled to the Consumer's Association. After that, we felt we'd done our part.

A quiet week followed. Jody's baby showed signs of producing a tooth, and I increased my morning run by ten minutes, but other than that we put one foot in front of the other in the usual way.

Then Jody called and told me she'd been seeing a van parked on the street outside her house.

"Is that really unusual?" I asked.

"It's unmarked, though."

"Which makes you think it's Mr. Li's?"

"It would make sense, wouldn't it? He's not going to drive around with a company name and number on the side of the van if he hasn't actually registered a company, is he?"

"You're right. But he's probably not the only one in town without a name on his van. Is there anybody in it?"

"I can't see anyone."

"Then it's not our guy. They just like that parking space."

"But—"

"Jody, it's not a threat if he's not making himself known."

Then Jody got up one night to settle the baby and looked out the window as she rocked her. The van was there. It was two a.m.

She called me at seven because she knows I'm up early.

"Look," she said, "we're leaving for Seoul tomorrow, for a week. Can you do me a favor and pick up our paper? I don't want it to look like there's no one home."

I never saw a van on the street when I went by for the paper, and I made a point of going by at different times of day in order to do a proper surveillance job. I can't say the absence of a van made me feel secure, though. There was no van in the parking space, but there was the very marked *atmosphere* of a van. A phantom van. A vantom. Because that's what a threat is. It's an idea. I never saw my stalker, but he was a poisonous cloud I could always smell. So even though the streets were quiet, fallen mangoes were rotting obediently, and nothing upset the cicadas, walking to and from Jody's house still put my hair on end.

Jody called the day she got back to thank me and get a report.

She called me the day after that to ask me to come over if possible because the van was outside her house again, and Mr. Li was sitting in it, staring her way.

The house is one street over from my condo, probably a four-minute walk. It turns out that she had called the police right after she called me. That's probably what gave her the idea that it would be safe to go outside and get the confrontation going. So as I walked up and heard their voices getting louder, a police car pulled up as well, and

Imran came out of the house. I was there to hear the police tell Jody that there was nothing they could do because the plumber wasn't physically on her property.

"He's threatening me, though!"

"He's on the other side of the gate."

They left.

Mr. Li looked at me and said, "Who are you? The bodyguard?"

"A witness," I said.

He looked all three of us in the eye and spat his next words out. "You don't know who I am. But they do. The police do. And they leave me alone."

I started looking at him more carefully then. No matter how hard I tried, I couldn't see his thick, oily hair and pocked face as important, but I know he certainly felt important.

"But what you do is illegal!" Jody blurted. Imran put a hand on her shoulder to rein her in.

"What I do is invisible. Not the same."

"But—"

Imran spoke up. "What exactly are you asking us to do?"

"You withdraw your complaint about me."

"Why? It's the truth!" said Jody.

"Because I know where you live. I know where your baby lives."

This was too much like the notes I used to get after

work. Apparently it pulled Imran's trigger as well.

If Imran alone had swung at Mr. Li, or if I alone had kicked him, I don't think there would have been an accident. But Imran punched at the same moment as I kicked, and Mr. Li flew backwards over my leg and into the street. The car that was barreling down the hill to catch the green light went right over him as if he were just one more speed bump and crushed his neck.

Jody started screaming, so the baby did too, and the driver of the car ran up and said, "Oh, my God, he can't be dead," and Imran took Jody's phone and pressed redial for the police. Then Jody took the baby inside the house. Imran and the driver and I said a few things, then stood speechless by the body. That was the moment, before the neighbors gathered and before the police came back, when everything was quiet, and Singapore felt safe again.

# The War
# Of The Worlds

Being on the couch with Mrs. Schumacher wasn't anything like being on the couch with Betty Riddle. For one thing, we were completely alone. That idiot Bert Guthrie wasn't peeking in the window to see how far I got. For two, Mrs. Schumacher was making me listen to classical music, and for the first time in my life it wasn't something people talked over.

I had dropped in to see if Walter was home. To get there I walked past the Hartmann house. As usual, Totsie and his brother Wolf were out in the yard shouting unintelligibly and trying to kill each other with pitchforks. I understood why my parents preferred it if I avoided them and their family. I didn't understand their reservations about Walter, though. He never picked a fight, and when he disagreed with you it was impossible to know it until you thought about the conversation later. Even so, this part of town, the area where most of the Germans lived, was the one area we didn't hang around in. It was too quiet, the kids all said. But it wouldn't have been quiet if we'd played there.

Walter wasn't home, he was helping out at his father's hardware store in Clayton, but Mrs. Schumacher invited me in anyway. She said, "Would you like to come in, Tom? I'm listening to some music." I didn't have anything to do, and the way her voice stayed level instead of rising into that range people used to be polite to children made me feel comfortable. I was fourteen, and the Nazis were about to take Paris.

The Schumachers' living room wasn't at all like ours. It was olive green and wooden and textured where ours was light blue and flowered and smooth. We both had pianos, but ours was a baby grand and it had photographs in silver frames all over it. Theirs was the concert version, and it was bare. Mrs. Schumacher went straight to the gramophone and picked up the needle to stop the music. "I imagine you thought I'd be listening to Wagner," she said in her gently accented way, "but today it's Verdi."

I'd never heard of either of them, so I kept quiet. She replaced the needle. "Come," she said, and we sat on the couch. She didn't turn toward me to make polite conversation but faced forward with her knees pointed at the gramophone, so I did the same. I tried to tune in to her, but she was tuned in to something else.

174

After a while I said, "I play the piano."

She said nothing for a moment, then said quietly, "So do I." She didn't look at me. A little bit later she said, "Verdi was a church organist at age seven." Many minutes passed before she said, "Listen to the clarinet." I played piano in a jazz band, so I could identify the clarinet easily. Our clarinet player's instrument never spoke as unforgettably as this one, though. In 1941, people weren't dancing slowly, at least not where we were playing, so his horn was a much more frivolous thing.

I had never heard music go on for so long before. Once it was finished, Mrs. Schumacher sat for a moment, so I did as well, and then I began to miss it. I honestly felt the echoes of the notes drifting slowly out the window, and it made me sad. Eventually she stood up, crossed to the gramophone and picked up the needle again.

I cleared my throat, and suddenly she spoke, as if I had been making noises about leaving. "I have one more thing to play for you. A little thing." She removed the Verdi, replacing it carefully in its sleeve like I did with my Tatum and Dorsey records, and replaced it with another. "There's another Italian you *must* hear." She looked at the sleeve for a moment, then placed the needle where she wanted it. It was a song. A woman sang, higher than the clarinet had, but just as profoundly. Mrs. Schumacher stood by the gramophone as we listened, then picked up the needle again when it was finished. "Alessandro Scarlatti," she said.

I nodded.

"Some people say that the Germans think a song is only good if it is difficult and that only the Italians know what a real song is."

An image flashed into my mind, and I'm sure I blushed.

Louie, our clarinetist, was Italian and represented all I knew of Italy. Just two days before, I had been sitting with him in the back of Joe the bassist's car on the way to a gig, and he said to the other guys, "What do you say we show young Tom here a slice of real Italian pizza?" Joe nodded with a laugh, and the guy sitting next to him, Frank the drummer, passed a photo back over the seats. I took it in my hands. It was a naked woman with her legs open. Her head was out of the picture; it was just the legs and what was between them. Whatever I had imagined to be between Betty's bobby socks and blouse when we were necking on her couch, this was not it.

Mrs. Schumacher still stood by the gramophone.

I cleared my throat again. "What do you think, Mrs. Schumacher?"

"I know what they mean," she said. "But they have forgotten Schumann."

I stood. At fourteen I wasn't quite as tall as my mother, but I was eye to eye with Walter's. She didn't put her hands on her hips or play with the pearls at her throat

176

like my mother did when she talked. She wasn't wearing pearls. In fact, I don't recall that she was adorned in any way, and her hands were at her sides. I said thank you, that was very interesting, and goodbye.

I have no idea what Mrs. Schumacher was thinking that day. I only know what I was. As I walked back home through the quiet German neighborhood—Totsie and Wolf were either dead or inside their house—I thought: I wonder if I have to go all the way into St. Louis to find some Schumann. Then I noticed the brick wall I had scooted behind three years before when I believed Orson Wells about the Martians and had run home from Walter's to save my mother. Then I thought: There's no way that Mrs. Schumacher or anyone's mother looks the way that photo did between the legs. Betty Riddle neither.

# Really Trying To Get Somewhere

We always sat in the front, Gray and I, whatever the vehicle. That time in Colombo, though, it wasn't until we finally pulled out of the train station that we realized the front was actually the back.

This time it was the seventy-five-year-old Viceroy, a train once gleaming and fit for the likes of Lord Mountbatten, and now a bit duller and fit for the likes of us: two dozen travel agents, guests of SriLankan Airlines. The windows were broad, and we could see what we were leaving behind. Outside, the beleaguered city baked. Arriving the night before, we had made out little on the way from the airport except roadside security checkpoints and lurid, illuminated statues of Jesus and the Buddha under glass. Within minutes now we were out of it once again, startling bony water buffaloes off their embankments and back into the fields.

Our hosts, the airline's PR team, passed around a

bottle of Johnny Walker Black and made it known that the party had begun and wasn't to end until Sunday night, two days away. I turned in my seat and leaned back against Gray. I thought it made us look cozy. When the bottle came around and it was our turn to drink from the cap, Gray spilled some on me as he poured. I laughed too loudly. I always do that. Sometimes he goes along with it, sometimes he winces.

Four Sri Lankan musicians trooped down the aisle and established themselves directly in front of us, propping their bums up against the air conditioners, which was excellent as it was growing very cold in the car. The leader of the group was a dead ringer for James Brown, in a knitted poncho rather than a cape. The other three had alarming overlapping teeth, and one had an Adam's apple that outdid his tambourine for attention. Gray smiled when I joined in with them on "Swing Low, Sweet Chariot."

They trooped back out again and I stood up to stretch, noticing that at least half of the other guests had also left. Someone in a car behind was playing "All of Me" on an amplified saxophone. Gray had taken out his book, and must've felt me looking at him. "Sit," he said, patting my seat. "Keep me warm."

I sat, and he put his left arm around me, reading again. I held his dangling hand and fiddled with his fingers for a while, looking at the battered-looking palms on either side of the receding tracks. Before long I felt trapped and jumped back up, heading out of the cool of our car and into the heat of the next one. A door immediately on the right revealed a mishmash of open flames and bubbling sauces presided over by a burly chef in a tall white hat. This car had windows that actually opened and a bar at the far end. Small tables with checkered cloths sat next to the windows and sported flowers in small vases that needed constant supervision.

The faces were redder in here, from the heat and the drink. The saxophone had been retired and the men were now singing the classics of Elvis Presley while the women hooted from along the sides. The train was extraordinarily slow but swayed vigorously. Vincent, one of our local hosts, was playing the guitar. His skin looked as if it would leave a glistening smudge if it rubbed yours, and you would want to lick it off.

Most of us had met only that morning in the lobby of the Colombo Hilton, but the feeling in the car was extremely open and comfortable. Two of the men actually had their arms around each other as they mangled the lyrics to "Love Me Tender." Apparently it was possible to be a successful travel agent and still let your hair down. I imagined we were letting our hair down, Gray and I, when we took exotic weekends away, but I was completely disarmed and excited when Sam, from one of the big London agencies, went down on one knee and took my hand, aping passionate devotion for the rest of

181

the verse. His curls bobbed fetchingly across his white English forehead.

Two songs later Vincent, Sam, a Dubai-based Brit named Jeremy and I were twisting to our own garbled reproduction of "Blue Suede Shoes." I had the soaring feeling I always experience when belting out a song. I often wondered privately if there were a type of orgasm that would be as joyful, but so far my climaxes with Gray had been merely lovely, and sometimes made me cry. Then someone poured beer on our heads.

Alone in the bathroom, washing my face and neck, I stared at myself in the mirror, less to check my appearance than my identity. *This is you, right?* I asked. *Right*, I answered back. *Where've you been?* I asked, but there was no answer. When I emerged, Gray was looking for me. "There are canapés if you're hungry," he said, raising an eyebrow at my new wet look.

Our quiet car was set for a delicate feast, and we were the first to arrive. The narrow table in front of each pair of seats had been covered in fresh white linen, and plates of pretty morsels awaited us. It felt as if something had gone wrong at a wedding and the luncheon was being foregone, but we were too polite to discuss it. I was hungry enough to put on a smile and dig in.

Eventually Jeremy and his wife, Justine, joined us, and we all accepted warmish white wine from the waiter. "Cheer-ho," Jeremy said to Justine, and she to him, and they drank with gestures that were possibly too often repeated in their life. Their pop eyes were red and watery, her chins were full and flowing, his belly in its floral print nudged the table for more space to itself.

Banana trees lined the tracks now, and sporadic communities. Every once in a while there were a few sturdy, painted houses with verandahs, potted plants, and a car. Otherwise we glimpsed only clay walls and corrugation in among the dense greenery. The children lounging in doorways waved, eyes bright and perfect, clothes dull and tattered. After we passed, people oozed onto the track from the safety of the foliage. No doubt it was the straightest path from A to B, and trains traveled slowly and infrequently enough for everyone to move aside in time. I waved, and elderly men in skirts and horn-rimmed glasses raised their ubiquitous black umbrellas in response.

Gray needed a nap, so I went back to the party car. Everyone still had a sweating beer in hand, but things had calmed down a bit and most people were sitting. The train had begun climbing into the hills of the tea country and the air was cooler, so I leaned out of the window next to Sam, who had been doing so long enough to sunburn his face. We looked in silence at the dripping wall of the hill we were hugging. As we pulled our heads in for a tunnel, Sam steadied himself with a hand on my arm. I thought with a pang of Gray alone in the dark.

Beyond the tunnel the vista opened up and from one side of the train we could see a valley so green with sun and tea that it felt sacred. If someone had invited me to walk in it, I might have refused. On the other side was a forest. Between the slender trees a waterfall cascaded slowly over lazy steps of deep, flat rock. Young women in pale saris stood midstream pouring water over themselves. I hurried back to Gray to see if he had noticed them as well. He had. "If you saw it in a brochure, you wouldn't believe it," he said. I sat down. It was exactly what I had been thinking.

Later, after a round of silly quiz games, we stopped in a station, apparently to let another train pass. I studied the words on the signs. The local script was tremendously artistic, even erotic. Perhaps the letters were rendered in the most uninteresting of official fonts, boring to Sri Lankans, but to me they represented nothing less than a series of taut scrota, broad buttocks, and perfectly rounded breasts. I pointed this out to Gray, and he smiled his half smile. He then turned around and repeated what I'd said to Friedrich, the wealthy, silver-haired CEO of Germany's oldest and most prestigious travel concern. Then he sat down again and opened his book. I was astounded. Half the time I didn't think Gray heard a word I said, and here he was doing publicity for me.

It was the eve of Sinhalese New Year, and the Sri Lankans on the platform were dressed for it. The older women wore saris, the older men were in white. Looking at the young women you would have thought the year was 1950, save for their hair. They favored the modest, full-skirted dresses of half a century before but kept their hair in braids, appearing painfully naïve. Whatever it was that was going to happen to them hadn't happened yet. And whatever it was would have something to do with the young men slouching in packs at the edge of the platform. They owned the place.

One of them, wearing the sleek, parted hairstyle of a bygone soda jerk, put out his cigarette with his foot, looked up, and caught my eye. *Now I own you, too*, his look said to me. His buddies watched as I allowed that he did, letting my eyes fall to my book, moistening my lips. When I looked up the boy hadn't moved a muscle. I smiled shyly and turned my eyes away. I'm good at this game; I've played it on more trains in more countries than I can list. Sometimes the men are outside the car, sometimes inside. Either way, it's dangerous if you play by the rules, which require escalation. If you appear too shy, they will not persevere. If you are immediately bold, you can stare them down, like a wolf in a power play, and the game is over. No, you have to show interest and disgust in just the right amounts, at just the right moments. By the time the Viceroy pulled out, the sultry boy and I had had each other, right there across Gray's book.

We pulled into Nuwara Eliya in the dark and were

185

directed onto buses in which we climbed further into the hills, slowing only slightly on the turns for approaching vehicles and awkward, sideways-running mongrels. We sat in the front, across the aisle again from Jeremy and Justine. Jeremy was asleep in a few minutes, snoring voluptuously. I checked Justine for signs of discomfort. She showed none, looking straight ahead as if she were alone in the world.

In the hotel foyer pretty women bedecked us with necklaces of hydrangea blossom and offered champagne glasses of small, deeply red strawberries. Waiters in white jackets came around with silver pitchers of thick, sweetened cream. "More," I said, every time they passed. We found our room and climbed under the cool, heavy covers of the big bed. I put a hand on Gray's warm softness but he didn't rise. He patted me a few times on the shoulder in the way he does, meaning, "Thanks anyway." We fell asleep as we always do, even if we're fighting, with the arch of my left foot on the top of his right one.

We were the first to make it to breakfast the next day, and burned our tongues on the curry we were served, dousing the flames with yogurt. Then we went outside. The morning was fresh and dewy and the setting, like the old hotel's whitewashed walls and dark exposed beams, reminded us of the Alps—our agency's specialty before we moved to Hong Kong. The hills surrounding us were a playground for sun and mist. Snapdragons lined the hotel garden—no doubt a British legacy—and a few cows grazed behind them. A toothless, shoeless old woman bundled in a frayed orange sari smilingly swept leaves from the path.

Gray walked the way he always walks, as if he's really trying to get somewhere. He's like a hunting dog sniffing the wind. I stopped to take a few photos—an elderly man reading his newspaper in the sun by a bright blue wall, a baby in a woolly cap in the arms of a young girl—and had to run to catch up.

"Why don't you wait?" I asked when I came up beside him.

"Why should I?" he asked me in his plain, matter-of-fact manner.

Sometimes he takes my breath away, and I wish he wouldn't. "Okay," I said, practically jogging at his side. "Which is harder to do, stop momentarily while a picture is taken, or run fifty feet?"

"That depends on who you are," he said.

Later that morning, we were escorted to the Governor's Cup, sponsored by the airline. During the thirty years of Socialist government in Sri Lanka, horse racing had been forbidden. Now they were off again.

Gray and I had been to the races in Kentucky, Hong Kong, Ascot, Penang, and Singapore. We'd never bet excessively, but we loved the animals, and many of our clients trusted us with the arrangements for their pilgrimages to the races, knowing that we had made

187

similar arrangements for ourselves. I talked to the hotels; Gray liked arranging transport.

The racetrack in Nuwara Eliya was absolutely charming, if you had no expectations. This was what I decided I would tell potential visitors if they were interested. We arrived about 9:30. The old stands had been newly whitewashed and trimmed in green. Up in the VIP section there was a steady flow of wine and beer, and below us on the grass were tables covered with chafing dishes full of deep-fried finger food. Further along were the stands for the masses, and in between, a pop band. I thought they were great and couldn't take my eyes off the lead singer, who was very tall and lanky, with a stud in his lower lip. To get his eyes on me, I danced in my beautifully tailored double-breasted suit and excellent broad hat. I had invited Gray to join me, but he didn't feel the need. Dozens of people watched as I kept my cool alongside the only other person willing to dance, a fellow wearing several mismatched shades of blue and possessing no sense of rhythm.

I noticed, when I checked, that Gray had a girl by his side. They were poring over the racing lineup together. He motioned to me, and I danced across the grass, climbing carefully over the rope that divided Them from Us. As I approached, I imagined this Sri Lankan teenager sitting on Gray's lap, toying with the buttons of the embroidered waistcoat we bought for him on a tour of Rajasthan. I did this sometimes, put strangers in the clinch with Gray. I tried to picture him doing different things with them than he did with me. In my mind, he looked delighted to have her in his arms, though I could tell he wasn't going to do a thing with her. Then I admonished myself. She really was very young. Maybe I should have paired him with Ranjika, one of the airline people. She had come to the races in a sari. Her lips were full and glossy, and a warm span of fat relaxed in the sun between her top and her skirt.

"This is Mumtaz," Gray said, beaming, indicating the girl. She was wearing jeans and a T-shirt and held a floppy pad of paper and a pencil. "She's going to help us pick the winners." He was drinking beer. I drank a beer myself while we watched our picks win the first two hilarious races. The furry little ponies scrambled around the course under oversized, long-haired jockeys in billowing silks. I drank another as Mumtaz helped us with the second two races as well. Somehow we only broke even, but we did a little celebratory hula for the astonished VIPs. I pointed to Ranjika. "What do you think of that, Gray?"

"Yum," he said, betraying nothing of the feeling on his face.

I got up on tiptoe and whispered in his ear, "Shall I get a sari?"

"No," he said, and I dropped back onto my heels. "White women don't look good in saris. They don't look good in kimono, they don't look good in cheongsam."

He was right, the bastard. That wasn't at all what he was supposed to say, but he was right. What you want is the real article. It's not the saris that make South Asian women so luscious; it's the other way around. Luscious ergo sari. Pandora's Box ergo kimono. Feline ergo cheongsam. Ball-breaker ergo tailored suit. And I had to admit I myself wouldn't really want Gray in a sarong so much as I'd want someone dark and unusual and familiar with curved knives and keening prayers.

In preparation for the Governor's Cup, for which they were going to bring out the serious horses, a bony woman with a basket over her arm went around the track dropping bits of turf into the holes left by the ponies' hooves, securing them there with a sandaled foot. Justine was standing on her own by the rails, watching the woman, and I went and stood beside her. I thought how nice we must look from the back, I in my trim skirt and she in her flowing one, both of us in our hats. I hoped someone would take a picture. When she looked at me, though, I felt a shock. There were broken capillaries all over her cheeks, and her watery eyes—the cracked blue of glaciers—jumped rapidly from side to side. For a moment I thought she might have just gone crazy that very minute, but she smiled calmly at me and pulled on her cigarette. A tray of wine appeared between us and we each took a glass of white. I knew it would give me a headache, and I knew that if Gray saw me drinking it after two bottles of beer he'd know it would give me a headache, but I didn't care. "Cheer-ho," she said, and I gulped about a third of my drink before speaking.

"Justine," I said, "remember when Jeremy was snoring on the bus yesterday evening?"

She laughed. "Yes."

"Were you embarrassed?"

She shrugged. "Not really. If I wake him he just falls asleep again and we're back where we started." She took a sip of her wine. "Why? Were you embarrassed for me?"

"No," I lied.

"We've been in Dubai so long," she said. "It's perfectly acceptable there."

"So is polygamy."

Justine shrugged again. "Some things you take, some things you leave."

We looked together at the hills behind the racecourse, and I noted the charcoal clouds that were darkening them. She seemed to be thinking hard, and spoke again. "You take what makes your life easier," she said. "How long have you been married?"

"Eight years," I told her, and she nodded as if this sounded about right for the way I was behaving.

Suddenly there was a thudding and a snorting, and the horses for the Governor's Cup were before us, parading to the gate. They were like lunatics being taken on an excursion, expressions unreadable, high stepping and sidestepping, wheeling and jumping.

"Magnificent," Justine said, when they had passed.

"Ninety percent pure energy, ten percent hoof and hair," I said.

The gate was halfway along the far straightaway. In the tension as the horses assembled, I asked her, "Have you ever had an Arab?"

I thought she would laugh again, but she didn't. Instead she grew wistful. "There was a beautiful fellow once, who paid me a lovely compliment." Then she pulled herself up and sniffed. "Looks like rain."

Back at the hotel, I found myself next to Jeremy at the buffet lunch on the covered porch. He knew precisely what he liked to eat, and while I took a little of every unidentifiable thing as an experiment, he piled his plate with rice, two kinds of the five curries, and marinated cucumbers extricated from between slices of tomato. "That should do me," he said happily. There was a *tap tap tap* on the roof of the porch, and big wet blotches appeared on the flagstones. "Perfect," Jeremy said. "I hope it lasts so I can sleep in the rain." We chose beers and went to join our spouses.

Gray was sitting with Friedrich at a dainty wrought-iron table in the middle of the lawn, under an umbrella. I huddled in with the two of them. Friedrich was talking about flying to the Maldives from Colombo when we got back. He had heard there wasn't much to do there, so he had brought along two enormous books to read and hoped they would be enough company. He looked serious and brave, and if Gray hadn't been there I'm sure I would have offered to go along and entertain him. Then Gray informed me, by way of speaking to Friedrich, "I'm trying to arrange to stay in Colombo for a few days."

The rain beat down harder as if to admonish Gray for telling me about it in this way, but he carried on eating.

"Ja?" said Friedrich. "You have business there?"

"I hope so," said Gray. "I want to talk to the people who charter the Viceroy. I think we can make it work as part of one of our packages." He put his knife and fork together on his plate and belched quietly, patting his stomach. "I need a nap," he said to us both. "Are you coming?" he asked me.

"Not yet," I said, even though my appetite was gone.

After he left, I stared at Friedrich.

"Business is good?" he asked me.

"Not bad." I felt the beer beginning to depress me. "I wonder how much it matters, though."

"Why?" he said evenly. Older people seemed to take everything in stride.

I shrugged. I didn't want to depress him as well. "Are you married?" I asked.

"I was," he said. "My wife died a few years ago."

"Oh, shit."

This made him laugh a little, but he'd clearly had enough. The rain began to let up. "If you'll excuse me," he said, "I will take a rest." He patted my knee as he stood to go and told me, "You're in Sri Lanka. Have a good time."

I also loved napping in the rain but I knew I wouldn't fall asleep today. And I knew Sam and his gang from London would be in the bar, maybe with some of the Sri Lankans as well. I went in search of them.

A roar went up when I entered the room, and immediately my spirits lifted. There were many glasses on the dark, shining bar, and the group was raucous. Sam stood up to give me his barstool and said, "You're on our team." Immediately I was told how to play the drinking game Vincent had introduced. It was very complicated and involved longer and longer strings of numbers. I survived for about a beer and a half before teaching everyone how to play quarters. Sam pulled an English one-pound coin out of his pocket, but it didn't bounce well. Someone came up with a Singaporean fifty-cent piece. It was a better weight, and flashed nicely in the lights over the bar. When Gray appeared in the doorway, I was showing the other fellows how I could roll the coin off my breast and still have it bounce into the shot glass.

"I'm thinking of going for a walk," he said from the door. "Would you like to come?"

"I would," I said. I couldn't possibly drink any more. When I jumped off the barstool it fell over backwards, but Sam caught it in one hand and saluted with the other as

I followed Gray out of the bar. I had to hold his arm to negotiate the steps out of the hotel, but then I let go.

"I thought you were coming for a nap," he said, sounding hurt.

"You thought wrong," I said, trying to make myself sound as plain and straightforward as he usually did, but sounding mean instead.

After a while I remembered why I was feeling snippy. "When did you decide to stay on in Colombo?" I asked him.

"Last night," he said, cool as a cucumber.

"I thought we were a couple, Gray," I said. "I would love to stay on in Colombo."

"I'm sorry," he said with a glance. "I thought it made more sense for you to get back."

You thought wrong, I thought, and I should have said so. I should have pursued it. But sometimes you don't say more because you don't want to hear more.

We walked toward the marketplace with bruises on our hearts, while around us a team of young men in matching satin jackets was handing out bumper stickers advertising a new Internet service provider. Across the pitted road, someone invisible in the dark of a narrow shack was grinding the spices that sat in open sacks on the sidewalk. The market began beyond the next intersection, but we could see from a distance that it featured mostly knock-off sporting goods and plastic toys. We passed a grim concrete church and turned left at the corner, following the road up a hill past the police station. Gray held my hand. When we passed the station gate with its barbed wire and its turret with evil slits for the guns of sharpshooters, I felt a chill go up both our spines.

We left the hubbub behind. I looked left and right at the bungalows lining the road. Gray appeared to be focused straight ahead, but when I pointed out to him a particularly charming if rundown bungalow or garden, he always acknowledged it as if he'd seen it already. He had registered it, perhaps he'd even felt something about it, but it hadn't warranted conversation.

The top of one hill was the foot of another. When the paved road ran out we took a grassy path even higher, weaving among the cowpats and looking down on the little gardens below us. No doubt the houses were damp and drafty, but the vegetables grew well. Gray pointed across the valley. "We could have a villa on that ridge," he said, but cold clouds rolled down and obliterated it from view as we watched. "Or not."

I wondered what we could have. I wasn't entirely clear on what we did have, particularly as my head was beginning to hurt, but I wanted to know what else was possible for us. If I didn't keep running to catch up, what would I lose? We headed back down. When we reached the paved road again we turned right in search of an alternate route back to the hotel. We passed what may have been a girls' school. A cluster of pretty round faces of all ages peered over the wall, taking in the holiday passersby. I smiled at them, and they were delighted. From somewhere in the back a voice called out, "See you tomorrow!" and the whole group dissolved into giggles. We turned left, interrupting a game of street cricket, then right again. Up ahead in the road stood about a dozen tall, teenage boys, interacting in a tight huddle outside a van emitting pop music with a heavy beat. As we came closer it was clear that some of them were dancing. They wore cargo pants or low-slung jeans, with unnecessary sunglasses resting on the backs of their necks. They would have looked just right in Los Angeles. More right than they looked on this quiet street between gardens of pink and yellow pansies.

They didn't move out of our path. Gray pushed his way through ahead of me and I felt the crowd begin to close behind him. I reached out a hand for him to pull, but he didn't look back. A few voices were saying, "Dance? Dance?" and an arm went around my waist from behind. It felt warm, and good. I liked the song coming out of the van; it was the kind of music I could dance well to. I began to sway, and the boy whose arm was around me pulled my body to his. I pushed back against him and bent my knees to rock from side to side. The alpha male, who wore beautiful gold earrings in both ears, looked me straight in the eye and put a thigh between mine, picking up on my rhythm as well. I raised my arms and some coward I never identified put a hand on my right breast. The circle around us grew tighter, and many of the boys began grunting their approval as the arm around my waist began traveling south. I kept my eyes on the eyes of the boy in front of me, as if all these arms and legs and hands really belonged to him. The whites looked yellow, the black irises infinitely deep and empty. He was going to have to move his thigh to accommodate the hand that was heading for my groin. The hand on my breast was performing an expert massage and began to flutter across my hardened nipple. There were fingers in my hair. When the boy behind me took hold of my throbbing crotch, the one in front pressed his thigh up against us both. I grabbed his shirt as if I wanted to strangle him. The crowd moaned. Then I shoved him backward. His groupies growled in protest, but he stepped aside and the crowd parted. Maybe he knew that Gray was watching from the corner.

I ran as steadily as I could along the road on legs made rubbery by the combined effects of alcohol, orgasm, and an eight-year-old fury. When I reached him I stopped and looked up into his pale face. "You see?" he said, shaking. "I *can* wait for whatever you have to stop and do."

Returning to our room, we passed the hotel gift shop, and I led Gray in. He followed without protest. I looked at some scarves, shuddering at their extreme softness. Gray stood in the middle of the shop with his hands on his hips, staring at the floor, while I cruised the edges. I didn't want this day to come to a screeching halt. I wanted to keep pushing at it. I found myself in the toiletries corner.

"Let's get some soap. I need a shower."

"There's soap in our bathroom," Gray said.

"They're not big enough." I took a gift pack of sandalwood bars to the cashier.

Upstairs we stepped into the shower and washed each other. Somehow we'd never done this before. We'd had sex in the shower, and we'd washed ourselves together in the shower on busy mornings, but we'd never washed each other. It was so sweet and peaceful, and neither of us did anything about Gray's arousal. When we'd dried each other thoroughly we climbed naked into bed. I don't know what Gray did or thought, but I turned on my side and slept like a baby until dinner.

The front seats were taken on the bus back to the station—Jeremy and Justine looked apologetic—as were the back seats on the train. On both vehicles, Friedrich sat behind us, reading one of his huge books. I liked having him there. For the first many hours of the trip we read too, and looked out at the tea. We were on the right side of the train to witness the rainbow of a distant storm. This was what Gray and I could do together. This, and organize wonderful tours.

After lunch the band got hooked up to an amplifier and began playing the same combination of Elvis and

World War I favorites we had heard on the way up. When we stopped for what seemed like days in a station, a boy tried to catch my eye. I gave him a look that said, "Not this time," and he winked at me and moved along the platform.

Later we drank tea in the bar car. Jeremy, on his umpteenth beer, had requested "Unchained Melody," and the bandleader found it somewhere in his dog-eared pile of music. When Jeremy began inverting the words I pushed into the rocking accordion between cars where the microphones were, and we howled the song together. Justine was nowhere near.

Afterward Gray and I found a relatively quiet corner and looked out the window. Darkness fell as we left the hills. White birds stood out in the gloom, leaping from the fields into the air and flying alongside us. Lightning flashed around the train, but no rain fell. As we eased past a small cement building with a peppering of teenage boys on its steps, one of them, inexplicably but comfortably clad in only a shirt and briefs, exposed himself to us. Gray threw a glance my way, and I smiled into the dark.

Closer to Colombo, more and more little houses appeared. The first were lit with kerosene, and the foliage around them was black, making the one bowl or cloth visible on the low table inside look like wealth. Later, there was fluorescent lighting and actual doors in the doorframes.

A bus took us to the Hilton, where Gray would stay on. I had to head almost immediately to the airport for my flight back to Hong Kong. Leaving him behind, I experienced the same pang that had gripped me when I thought of him on his own in the tunnel, but I didn't want to stay.

There was checkpoint after checkpoint as my taxi drove out of the city, where soldiers inspected every pocket of the car rather than my bags. Only one inquired as to what was in my hatbox, more out of curiosity than concern.

"Very strange box," he said.

"It's made especially for the hat," I told him, lifting the lid to give him a peek.

He leaned down to look inside and nodded.

"Put it on," he said.

"What?"

"It doesn't look nice?"

"No, it does. It's a great hat, but—"

"Put it on."

The taxi driver was waiting a little nervously. I guessed he needed me to do the right thing.

I pulled the hat from the box and put it on, tipping my head back quite far in order to look at the soldier from under the big navy brim. "How's that?"

He looked at me in frank appraisal, and nodded. "Yes. Okay. You can go."

The driver put the car in gear and we pulled out. As we did I heard the guard laugh, and felt his teeth flashing in the dark long after the rest of him had disappeared.

Thanks (in order of appearance)

Valerie Lester*
James Lester*
Toby Lester*
Alan Hodges
Alicia Erian*
Philip Tatham
Evelyn Somers Rogers*
Meira Chand*

*Read them too!